# AR

# The Beasts of Loch Ness

Mark A. Cooper

## Dedication

*To Sandra, thank you for the life we share.*

ISBN-13: 978-1979337380
ISBN-10: 1979337381

# Prologue

He inched to the edge of the lichen-covered boulder and threw a flat pebble into the loch. His mother had once shown him how to skim a pebble across the water at a beach, and Archie fondly remembered how skillful she was at it, her pebbles always dancing across the water's surface like a ballet dancer across a stage. Her secret: find one as flat as possible.

After a few attempts, he managed to skim one across the surface of the loch. It only bounced three times, but he was content with the knowledge that if she could see him now she'd no doubt be proud of him. Still grieving the loss of his mother, he gazed down into the deep water and looked at his reflection. His glasses slid down his nose, and using his forefinger, he pushed them up.

Something moved just below the surface. Archie could have sworn it was a pair of eyes looking up at him. Then, he saw them again.

"Mom," he whispered. A pair of orange eyes were watching him, but without warning, they disappeared. He shrugged it off. *It must just be my own reflection*, he told himself.

Looking around for more pebbles, he noticed one nestled between the boulder he was standing on and a smaller boulder against the water's edge. As he leaned forward, his heavy backpack slipped up to his neck, throwing him off balance. He toppled forward, his breath stuck in his throat and every muscle in his body tensed as he tumbled, grasping at air. He plunged headfirst into the murky depths, the water so cold it was like being struck with a baseball bat. His coat and clothing quickly absorbed the water and pulled him deeper below the surface. For the briefest of moments, he was paralyzed by the cold, before coming to life, fighting for survival. Running out of air, he shrugged off his backpack and kicked as hard as he could to the surface. Everything around darkened as he lost his bearings.

A terrifying deduction! Was he swimming towards the surface or going deeper? Archie panicked, wanting to scream for help. He was desperate to gasp air and fill his lungs. In total darkness, the water grew colder.

Then, he felt something catch his ankle and hold tight. His first thought was he was being rescued, and then an immobilizing fear came over him. He was being dragged deeper. He fought with everything he had as he was swept away in the underwater darkness. His arms thrashed and he kicked the object, but its grip was a vice. The darkness submerged his thoughts. His oxygen levels completely expired.

"Mom," he cried with his last breath of air.

*

Archie shivered. He lay on his side on what felt like a cold, wet rock. He opened an eye just a slit so he could peek. A strange bluish light all around him, he sensed something walking towards him, surrounding him from all sides. He tried to focus. He'd lost his glasses. Keeping his eyes almost closed, he pretended to be unconscious. If he was going to be eaten, he wasn't sure he wanted to see by what.

As he lay shivering from the cold and fear, he tried to block out the strange sounds and the abnormal footsteps approaching him. He found himself recalling the events of the week leading up to his arrival in Scotland. Looking back on it now, he supposed it had all started two weeks earlier after swimming practice . . .

# Chapter One

Imran Akran slid across the back seat of his mother's car. Archie Wilson jumped in next to him. The two ten-year-olds clicked their seatbelts on, extra careful not to damage their precious ten-meter swimming certificates and badges.

"I can't wait to show my mum," Archie said, reading his certificate for the fortieth time. "I don't think she really thought I could do it." Seeing his own name in big letters on the certificate was uplifting.

"Mom, please, can you sew my badge on my coat so I can wear it to school tomorrow?" Imran asked his mother.

Mrs. Akran started the engine and smiled at her son in the mirror. "Not tonight, but I will." She paused as she concentrated on driving. "Archie, will your mum sew yours on your school coat for you?"

"She said she would. I want to get the twenty-five meter badge next."

"Yeah, then one-hundred. We could have a coat full of badges," Imran said.

"I wonder how many badges we can get?" A broad smile stretched over Archie's face.

Mrs. Akran and Archie's mum took turns each week taking the boys to swimming club. Archie and Imran had been best friends since first grade. They lived just a few houses apart and often played together after school and at weekends.

Archie wore small half-framed glasses that partially hid dark eyebrows above large brown eyes. He was lanky and good-looking, in a relaxed, awkward sort of way, with tousled brown hair. At four feet four inches, he stood an inch shorter than Imran. An inch might not sound much, but it can make an awful lot of difference when you don't have many to spare.

Imran was the youngest of three boys. His parents spoke with strong Pakistani accents and mostly wore traditional Pakistani clothing. Imran's father always wore a turban. Imran, on the other hand was completely Westernized. He spoke with a Cockney accent and wore the latest and coolest clothing available.

"I wonder why Steven wasn't at swimming club tonight," Archie wondered, cleaning his glasses on his sweater before popping them back on again.

"He's caught bronchitis," Mrs. Akran said.

Imran thought for a second before replying. "I would like to catch a dinosaur too. I wonder what he feeds it."

Archie's face looked as if he was in pain before he burst out laughing. "Imran, you're tragic. Bronchitis is like a bad cold. It's not a type of dinosaur."

Both boys had a fit of giggles over the

it stopped abruptly as they approached Archie's home. Mrs. Akran slowed down. The tell-tale sign of flashing blue lights filled the car. A police car was parked where Archie's mom normally was.

"Look, a cop car outside your home. They're gonna arrest you for being tragic and cheating. You put your foot down when you were swimming," Imran said, laughing.

"I didn't put my foot down. I almost did but I kept going until I touched the side." Archie strained to look out the window, sliding his glasses up on his nose with his forefinger.

Mrs. Akran parked her car and wrapped her Bokitta scarf around her head. She wore Western clothing most of the time, but liked to wear the traditional Pakistani headscarf in public. They climbed out and walked towards Archie's home.

"I bet someone stole your mom's car," Imran said. "I saw it on TV. 'Joy riders' they call 'em. I bet they wrecked it. Probably rolled it over and it burst into flames. Boooooooookkkkkkssssshhhh." Imran made a crashing sound.

As they approached the house, Archie felt a twinge of apprehension. A policewoman and a policeman stood at his front door.

The policewoman noticed them and walked down the steps to meet them in the street. "Can I help you?" She had bushy brown hair that looked like it was trying to escape from under her hat.

"Hello. I'm Mrs. Akran. We live at number sixty-seven. I took Archie swimming. Is everything all right? Where's Mrs. Wilson?"

The policeman joined them. "Can I have a word with you alone, please?" he said to Mrs. Akran. "Boys, stay here with Constable Fletcher for a minute."

Mrs. Akran and the policeman went into the street to talk. Archie and Imran stayed with the policewoman he had called Constable Fletcher.

"Was it joy riders?" Imran asked excitedly.

"Sorry. What was?" Constable Fletcher asked.

Archie's attention was with Mrs. Akran and the policeman. Mrs. Akran looked distressed; they both looked back at Archie. He watched tears trickle down the face of his friend's mum. That was the moment Archie Wilson's world fell apart.

Everything became a blur to him. He spent the night at Imran's home, as he had many times before. But this was different. There would be no sneaking candy to bed. No soda hidden in Imran's closet. No flashlights for making animal shapes on the ceiling, and he wasn't in the mood for playing Xbox. Everyone was being exceedingly nice to him and spoke to him like he was a three-year-old.

The news that his mother had been killed by a drunk driver hadn't yet sunk in. Archie hoped that at any second the doorbell would ring and his mom would come and collect him. Imran did his best to comfort his friend, but when one's whole world disintegrates, there is nothing someone can do or say to help heal the pain.

\*

Social services uncovered who Archie's father was. Archie had never met him and knew nothing about him. His name was Alec McIntosh, and he lived in Foyers, Scotland. He worked as a boat mechanic by day and helped out behind the bar most nights at the White Stag Inn.

## Chapter Two

The pale blue Ford Fiesta twisted its way through the narrow lanes from Inverness, Scotland. Glenn Andrews was a social worker for Inverness County Council. He preferred the city life and what it had to offer but couldn't help being impressed by the stunning rugged scenery as he drove to Foyers.

Mile after mile, the soaring peaks, peppered with granite boulders on which sheep grazed, tickled the passing low clouds. As he rounded a corner, Glenn saw it in all its glory. He slowed his car and looked on in awe at the scene: Loch Ness, the largest volume of freshwater in the British Isles, containing more water than all the lakes, rivers, and reservoirs in England and Wales at over twenty-three miles long and nearly seven hundred and fifty feet deep. If you stood seventy-two school buses on top of each other and stood on the top, you would still get your feet wet. The massive lake radiated an innocent charm and deep mystery.

Glenn arrived at his destination and noticed an old man with large bushy sideburns that hung down to his shoulders walking with a *shillelagh,* a stout walking stick cut out from a tree, the handle a large wood knot. Shorter versions were used as clubs. When swung at force the shillelagh did considerable damage, especially if they connected to a man's head.

Glenn asked the old man for directions, and he pointed his shillelagh at the small boatyard on the side of the loch at Foyers. Confident with his new direction, Glenn drove towards the small boatyard and stepped out. It was a small building on the edge of the loch, large enough for two small boats to be stored and repaired.

"I'm looking for a Mr. McIntosh . . . an Alec McIntosh, to be precise. I was told I would find him here?" Glenn asked a man in dark blue overalls working on a small boat.

The man in overalls studied Glenn. He knew most people in Foyers, and most cars, so this was either a tourist or someone trying to sell him something. "Who's asking?"

Glenn stepped forward and read the name "McIntosh" on the breast pocket of the overalls. "Oh, are *you* Mr. McIntosh? Alec isn't it?" Glenn shuffled forward and took out his business card.

"Yes. But whatever you're selling, I'm not interested. I have work to do." Alec wiped his hands on his overalls before taking the card and reading it.

Alec McIntosh was a slim, good-looking man, with a rugged appearance and a boyish face. His jet-black hair was tousled as if he had just woken up. His deep blue eyes darted across the business card. "Social services?" Alec asked. "What do you want me for?"

Glenn informed him he had a ten-year-old son and explained everything about Archie Wilson. Partway through, Alec sat on a tire, looking up at Glenn in disbelief. He looked like a child himself, learning the facts about a son he never knew he had.

"That's why I don't go to football matches anymore, nothing but trouble," Alec said in his broad Scottish accent.

"Sorry. Football? What has that got to do with Archie?"

"Scotland was playing England at Wembley Stadium in London. A crowd of us from Foyers took the train from Inverness down to London for the weekend to support Scotland." Alec stood and rubbed the stubble on his chin. "I ended up staying for a month because I met this lass down there. I was only nineteen. She was about the same age. We thought we were in love, but I needed to get back to Foyers to work. She didn't want to move up here, and it seemed pointless going on together so we split up. She never called me."

"Did you ever call her?" Glenn asked before stopping himself. "Sorry that's none of my business. The point is you are Archie's only relative."

## Chapter Three

Alec lived alone in a small cottage on the edge of Loch Ness and worked nights at the White Stag Inn. Alec was like a son to the owners of the inn, Jack and Peggy Macdonald. His own mother had died when he was eighteen. Many knew the truth that the Macdonalds were getting too old to run the cozy country pub. Without Alec's help, they would probably have had to close up.

Just after eleven, when the last guest left, Alec bolted the door shut. He picked up a few empty glasses and walked back to the bar. Peggy watched him and could sense something was bothering him. "Alec, are you unwell? You don't seem yourself?"

Alec poured himself a glass of cider and sat down heavily on a barstool. He explained everything to Peggy regarding Archie. He went on to say he couldn't possibly look after a child, and it would be better all-round if Archie stayed in London with foster parents, close to friends and everything he knew. Yes, that would be the best for the wee lad, Alec noted.

The sympathy Alec expected never came. Peggy launched into him, telling him in no uncertain words that he had a responsibility and must take in his son. If he refused, he should move away from Foyers, for she would not want to know him if he failed his responsibilities. Alec had seen Peggy get angry a few times in the past before but couldn't remember seeing her so infuriated.

The following morning, he called Glenn, and arrangements were made for Archie to come to Scotland.

*

Archie had gone into a glum slumber, hardly speaking more than one or two words to anyone when he was informed he would be going to Scotland to live with his father. Archie's mum had told him very little about his father, and every time, it was a different story. When he was much younger, she told him his father was a soldier. Another time, he was a fireman. Another time, when he was watching a movie about the birth of Jesus and the narrator explained the Virgin Mary was given a child by God, his mother remarked, "Just like you Archie, a gift from God." After that, Archie stopped asking about his father.

Nothing seemed to concern Archie. He was deeply depressed. Scotland could have been on the next street or halfway around the world. It was a pitiful sight. Every time a car door slammed shut outside, he ran to the window hoping to see his mom getting out of her car to collect him. His world was in ruins.

Now he had gone to just staring out the window. It was horrible outside. The grey clouds stretched across the sky. Raindrops chased each other down the glass. It was hard to say what was more downcast, the weather or Archie.

## Chapter Four

Archie and Imran waited with Mrs. Akran in an interview room at social services. Archie was not sure if he felt excited or nervous to see his father for the first time. He was hoping it would be over soon. Since his mother's death he decided he didn't like the social services people. They spoke to him as if he was a baby. *I'm ten and a half and big enough to do what I want,* he told himself.

The door opened and two men walked in and looked at the two boys. Archie studied them. One was thin with wire-rimmed glasses perched on a long nose. He was about forty and was wearing a cheap crumpled suit that looked like it had been slept in. Archie couldn't see his mum liking the man much.

Archie was more interested in the other man. Although, at first, Archie thought he was too young to be his dad, wearing black pants and pale blue sweater and seemed to be just as nervous as Archie. He looked out of place.

"Hello, Archie," the thin man started. "I'm Glenn Andrews from Inverness Social Services. You'll get to know me quite well as I'll be checking on your progress."

Archie and Imran looked wide-eyed at each other without speaking. Glenn had a strong Scottish accent. In normal circumstances, they would have probably laughed and mimicked him.

"And this Archie is Alec McIntosh, your father."

His father shook Archie's hand, and Archie noticed his father's palms were sweaty. He was not sure who was more nervous—him or his father.

"It's nice to finally meet you Archie. I'm looking forward to getting to know you," Alec said with a broad Scottish accent.

The room fell into an awkward silence before Archie eventually spoke. "This is Imran. He's my best friend. And this is his mum, Mrs. Akran."

After a few minutes of uneasy noncommunication, Archie finally said a tearful goodbye to Imran. His father carried Archie's bag, collected two large boxes from Mrs. Akran's car, and loaded up a small van.

The van only had two seats. Archie was pleased to be sitting in the front. His father gave him a cushion to sit on so he could see out the window. "You'll be wanting to be comfortable, Archie. We have a long drive. It took me over ten hours to drive here. I hope the traffic is better for our trip."

"Does the radio work?" Archie asked, pushing the buttons on the car radio.

"Nah, that old thing hasn't worked for years. Don't you have one of those 'I' things to play music? I thought all kids had them."

"No I don't. Imran has one," Archie said, "and it's called an iPhone. Don't you have an iPhone?"

" Me? iPhone? Nah, I'm not into modern gadgets. Give me an engine, and I can make it work. But all that iPod, iPad, iPhone stuff is too complicated. I use a regular phone." He showed Archie his flip cell phone. Archie sighed and using his middle finger pushed his glasses up on his nose.

The ten-hour drive seemed to take a week. Archie lost count of how many times they stopped for gas, or how many times he dozed off to sleep.

Archie watched the scenery flash by and never paid much attention during the journey. He counted the dead bugs squashed against the windshield. When they came to Foyers, his father remarked they were just a few minutes away from his cottage.

When they stopped at a stoplight, Archie's attention was drawn to a large church on the other side of the street. There was nothing unusual about the church at first glance, but as he continued to look at it, he noticed four large gargoyles sticking out from the rooftop. Archie had seen gargoyles before—many of the churches and even the town hall near his old London home had them on their rooftops. The grotesque creatures were carved of limestone and looked like monsters made up of half-lion, half-bear, or part-human, and some even with the heads of serpents. Usually large fangs dropped from the open mouths, which were sometimes used as water spouts to allow rainwater to drain from the roof.

To Archie, these looked different from those he'd seen before. Those looked scarier with menacing teeth and eyes, some with a clawed paw extended as if ready to pounce on passersby. The gargoyles on Foyers's church roof looked like *they* were scared, terrified rather than terrifying. The clawed paws stood as if protecting from a greater beast.

"Mr. McIntosh. Why are the gargoyles like that?" Archie asked his father.

"So, you do speak," his father said. "You know you can call me 'Dad,' or 'Alec' if you want."

Archie continued to look up at the gargoyles. "They look different. Why?"

His father quickly looked up. "I had-nee noticed them before." The light changed to green, the van moved off, and Archie craned his neck to get a last look. A few minutes later, Archie could see Loch Ness.

"Is that the Ocean?"

"Och, no laddie. It's Loch Ness, where Nessie lives," his father joked stopping the van by the cottage.

"There's no such thing as the Loch Ness Monster," Archie said matter-of-factly.

"Oh, and how do you know that?"

"You have lived here all your life. Have you seen it?"

"No, but strange things happen to you living at the loch," his father said, climbing out of the van.

"Like what?" Archie asked.

"Well, I haven't seen it, but plenty have . . . Here we are, Archie. Home, sweet home."

Archie looked at the small granite brick cottage. It sat in solitude just forty feet from the water's edge of Loch Ness. His father pointed further along the bank to a small building with a faded sign. "McIntosh Boat Repairs." This was where Alec Macintosh worked during the day.

Alec opened the front door, bent down, and picked up a handful of mail. Archie followed him inside.

"Mostly junk mail and bills," Alec said throwing the mail on the table. "Well, what do you think of your new home?"

Archie smiled, saying nothing. The cottage was small but clean. The ground floor had one room—a kitchen at one end, a large fireplace at the other. A small kitchen table with a couple of chairs stood in the center, towards the fireplace, where a gas fire hissed heat. There was also a black leather armchair. Archie was pleased to see a large TV on the other side of the room.

"Ah, well, you'll get to liking it I'm sure." Alec went back outside to collect Archie's things.

Archie followed a narrow staircase up and found the bathroom. He stuck his head inside and was pleased to see the toilet seat was left up. His mother had always nagged him about leaving it up. At least his father wouldn't say anything. This was a plus. Suddenly, Archie felt guilty for thinking like that. He paused and looked at himself in the mirror. He removed his glasses and wiped his eyes. Would he always feel like this whenever he thought of his mum? After wiping his nose on his sleeve, he popped his glasses back on.

The first bedroom contained a double bed, and some of his father's clothes hung over a chair. The second room was tiny: a small bed sat squat between the walls with a dresser opposite. Archie could just squeeze between to get to the window. He glanced outside. The view was impressive. From high up, he could see more of the loch. It was much larger than he first thought. He could just make out the shoreline on the other side, but to his left it seemed to go on endlessly.

"So you found your room okay. I guess you found the bathroom?" Archie jumped at Alec's voice

"Em. Yes, thanks," Archie said.

Alec sat on the bed and gestured for Archie to sit next to him. Archie sat down and looked at his father.

"I understand this must be difficult for you, Archie. You don't know me or Scotland. You've been taken away from your home, your friends, and lost your mother." Alec sighed, putting his arm around Archie. Archie stiffened. "It's not easy for me either, laddie. I never knew about you until a week ago. Now I find I have a son and have to bring him up? I'll be honest. I'm a lousy cook, I have no clue what music, food, or TV programs you like, and well, bringing up someone is going to be a challenge. But I promise you I will do my best by you. I take it you get yourself washed and dressed?"

Archie nodded. "I'm ten-and-a-half. I'm not a baby."

"Yes, of course. I'll take you to school tomorrow and get you settled in. I will see about a babysitter."

Archie frowned.

"A sitter I meant. You're not a baby. I work most nights at the pub. I can't leave you alone at night." He raised his eyebrows. "Can I?"

"What time do you start work?"

"I normally pack up the repair shop around five, take a shower, and head over. Of course, now I will pack up at four, and we can get dinner together."

"I'll be fine if you connect my Xbox up to the TV. Sometimes Mum had to pop out to get something from the store or see the neighbors, and I never burnt the house down." Archie suddenly felt sad again as he mentioned his mom. His eyes welled up and his bottom lip quivered.

His father hugged him tight. "Well, we'll see how we get on." The hug lasted just for the briefest of moments, but Archie felt better for the intimate contact. He wouldn't admit it yet, but he liked his father.

*

Later that night, Archie lay in bed staring at the ceiling. Then it suddenly struck him: the silence. A silence so profound it frightened him. A silence so intense and overpowering. Archie immediately sat up and clicked his fingers. *I'm not deaf,* he thought as he climbed out of bed and made his way to the window. The ten-hour journey with the drone of the car's engine and the whoosh of the wind rushing past were gone. But so was the strident symphony of London, the trains always in the distance, and the constant rush of London traffic. Gone were the car horns, the squeals of buses and taxis. Tonight, the world Archie knew was replaced with a tranquil yet deafening silence.

The loch shone peacefully with the powerful moonlight, reflecting its light across the hills and tree-lined banks into hollows and crevices, projecting an eerie shadow. Archie looked at the calm water and felt strangely drawn to it yet fearful of what secrets might lie beneath.

# Chapter Five

Foyers Primary School was tiny compared to any school Archie had seen before; even his old nursery school was larger. The school had two classrooms, the larger of which also used for assemblies, the school library, and the gymnasium. The school employed two teachers and just seventeen children between the ages of five and ten were enrolled. Once the students turned eleven, they attended Inverness Secondary School, a twenty-mile bus trip away. The classes were into two groups, ages five to seven and ages eight to ten. In London, Archie's class had thirty children, and they were all his age.

He walked to school with his father. Everyone knows that pain that develops in the stomach as a tight knot starts to form. Archie wouldn't know anybody and nobody knows him. The summer had fully extinguished itself. Early Scottish mornings in November had arrived, bitter winds blasted across the loch, bringing a wintery slap to exposed faces and hands.

"Is it always this cold here?"

"Aye, it is that," his father said, breathing out a heavy fog. "But you'll soon toughen up."

They were met by the headmistress, Mrs. Taggert, a plump lady with a round face. Archie tried counting her chins. Was it four or five? He couldn't be sure; when she looked down at him, it looked more like ten. She had a stern face, and Archie knew she was not someone to cross.

"Hello, Mr. McIntosh." She shook Archie's father's hand. "And you must be Archie McIntosh?" She smiled.

"No, I'm Archie *Wilson*." Archie was unsure if he should shake her hand or not. When she didn't offer it, he adjusted his glasses with his finger.

Another teacher, Mrs. Duncan, broke the awkward silence by ringing a hand bell, signaling time for school. Archie disliked walking into the new school, unsure what was worse, being ignored or stared at.

After a formal introduction to the class, the teacher instructed Archie to sit next to Chloe, who was ten and immediately informed Archie that she didn't like boys. Archie ignored her. The strong Scottish accents from the teachers and his classmates took a little adjustment.

All the children in the school had been born in Foyers. Archie felt as if he was crashing a party. As the day went on, most became more welcoming. Chloe was helpful; she was good at math and explained the school routine.

A contagious elation swept across the class when the large clock struck four. Archie was bewildered. The home he knew and loved was hundreds of miles away. A few parents picked up their children from school, but most children walked home.

"Archie, are you coming?" Chloe asked

"Where?"

"I live near you. We can walk together."

Archie nodded and studied her. She was a pretty girl with short dark hair and sapphire blue eyes; her rounded cheeks were lightly splashed with a few freckles. He walked alongside her looking at the various landmarks she pointed to.

"Do you have any brothers and sister?" she asked.

"No."

"I do. Evan is thirteen and goes to Inverness Secondary School." She passed him a mint.

"Thanks." Archie popped the mint into his mouth so he could bury his hands in his pockets again. He wondered why she was not shivering like he was. Maybe his father was right, and he would toughen up.

They passed a rickety stone cottage that sat on the edge of the loch. Chloe walked on the furthest edge of the path, keeping her distance from it as they approached.

"Hurry past here."

Archie almost had to run to keep with her. As they passed, he noticed an elderly man sitting on a rock next to the cottage. His face was covered in a wild bush of grey sideburns so long Archie had to take a second look or he would have thought it was a beard. Matching grey hair stuck out from under a tartan cap. He turned and stared at the two children. The man had black piercing eyes that were cold and empty. A shiver ran down Archie's spine. "That old man is creepy," he whispered.

"That's Mr. MacGregor. My mum said he always watched her when she was a little girl. He gives us all the creeps. Even my grandmother said he used to scare her."

Archie jogged to keep up. Something she had said didn't seem to add up. He thought maybe he misheard and ignored it. Although he could almost feel the old man's eyes burning into his back.

"We heard your mum and dad were divorced. I expect you're still sad about your mum?" Chloe asked. "Why haven't you been to visit your dad before? And why are you called 'Archie Wilson' and not called 'Archie McIntosh,' like your dad?"

Archie didn't answer. He was relieved to see his father's boat garage. "I'll see you tomorrow, Chloe." Archie walked towards the building.

"Bye." She smiled, watching him walk away.

Alec worked on a boat engine clamped to a bench. He nodded when he noticed his son walk in. "I see you met Chloe. Nice girl from a nice family. The Stewarts. I don't care too much for the job her father does, but he seems decent enough."

"She's a bit tragic and a nosey parker."

"Is that anyway to speak about a new friend who walked you home?"

"She was going this way anyway."

"No, son. She lives in East Foyers. She must have taken a fancy to you."

Archie couldn't work out if she was being friendly or just being nosey.

"You look frozen Archie. Get home. I'll be home soon. We'll have dinner at the pub tonight. My friends want to meet you."

Archie turned to walk away and stopped short to look at his father. "Um. Mr. McIntosh, is it okay if I get a drink from the fridge when I get there?"

Alec stopped what he was doing and walked towards Archie, wiping his hands on an oily rag. "It's not *there*. It's your home now and, Archie, if you don't want to call me 'Dad,' 'Alec' will work just fine. Get yourself anything you want from the fridge, son. I'll see you in a bit when I get home."

Archie nodded and turned. He walked alongside the loch towards the cottage. A few boulders jetted out into the water. He picked up a handful of pebbles and climbed onto a lichen-covered boulder were it all began. All Archie remembered was slipping into the loch and getting pulled down under the water . . .

# Chapter Six

As he lay shivering from the cold and fear, Archie tried to block out the strange sounds and the abnormal, approaching footsteps. Then he heard the most peculiar voices. He kept his eyes shut tight.

"Is it dead?" a high-pitched voice said in an outlandish Scottish accent.

"Let me tell you something. It's not an *it*, it's a human," came a deep voice from something so close to Archie he could feel it on his skin. The voice was like a foghorn, yet adolescent.

"We're doomed, Gordon. The humans have found us. Doomed we are," the first voice said.

"Let me tell you something. I don't think we are doomed. This is just a child, a boy. He looked so sad earlier, gazing into the loch."

Something pressed Archie's cheek. It felt like a rubber pencil eraser. At first, he ignored it, keeping his eyes closed, afraid to open them. Until it pushed again.

"Don't kick him," Gordon said.

Archie opened his eyes.

"Agh! It's alive. We're doomed!" the high-pitched voice said.

Archie lifted himself up onto one elbow, certain he was dreaming. Little furry creatures, no more than ten inches tall, surrounded him. At first glance, they looked like guinea pigs, but as he took a second look, they were like nothing he'd seen before.

Hundreds of the little furry creatures—all the size of a woman's purse—surrounded him. Mostly they were white, but some had black streaks of fur, others brown spots. They had two legs no more than four inches long and two little arms with three-fingered hands. When they blinked their eyes or closed their mouths, they looked lifeless.

"We thought you were dead," a little creature said in a French accent.

"I wish he was. Humans eat us. We are doomed. Doomed, I tell ya," the Scottish creature said, his voice wavering.

"What *are* you?" Archie asked, his eyes wide open in disbelief. He realized he had lost his glasses. The figures further away were harder to see.

"Not dinner, so you can get that out of your head," the French-sounding one said with a slight sneer and a piercing look.

"No. I won't hurt you."

"We are sporrans," said the Scottish one, sounding less gloomy. "Well, actually, we are the very last of our kind."

"No thanks to you humans and the gargoyles," the French sporran said.

"What's your name? I'm Jock." The Scottish sporran walked forward and held out his hand.

Archie gingerly took the little hand, which felt like a gummy bear. "I'm Archie Wilson, nice to meet you, Jock." Archie smiled and looked at the French-sounding sporran. It had longer eyelashes and scarlet lips, and appeared slimmer than some of the others. "And what's your name?"

"I'm Marlene Bardot. I came from Notre Dame in France. Many French sporrans fled eight hundred years ago. France was overcome with gargoyles, so we came here seeking shelter and help from Gordon," she said in a very posh French accent.

"How old are you?" Jock asked Archie.

"Um. I'm ten-and-a-half."

The sporrans chuckled among themselves until a taller, fatter sporran with grey fur approached. "Nice to meet you, Archie. Allow me to introduce myself. I'm Llewellyn, originally from South Wales. We, too, came here to seek protection from Gordon. I'm the head sporran. I have never met a human before. We spend most of our lives avoiding them."

"Why? We won't hurt you." Archie sat up and crossed his legs.

"Maybe not you, Archie, but over eight hundred years ago, sporrans roamed the world and lived in peace. Then gargoyles started to spread from Asia and—" Jock said and took a deep breath, "—they think we make a nice snack. Rumors that Gordon could turn them to stone spread across the world, so sporrans from all around the world came to Scotland to live in peace."

"Then how come I've never heard of you?" Archie asked.

"Huh, that's when the humans thought sporrans would make good food as well. They caught us, killed us, and used our stomachs to make something called a haggis, which they ate for dinner. They used our fur to make purses to hang from their kilts. You see, they have no pockets in kilts and the male humans needed somewhere to carry money or valuables. So, they used the skin of sporrans. We are the only sporrans left in the world now, and we live down here with Gordon."

"Who's Gordon?" As soon as Archie asked, he wished he hadn't. The sporrans all looked up over Archie's head.

"Let me tell you something. I'm Gordon. It was I who saved you from drowning. I noticed you before, looking into my loch with sadness in your eyes," the deep adolescent voice said from behind him.

Archie turned and, to his horror, standing right behind him was a massive creature. Its head was larger than a car, and each tooth as large as his father's hand. It stood over thirty feet tall, larger than two school buses on top of each other, and had a long spiky tail. Gordon had bright, orange, piercing eyes and primitive armour skin that looked rough, like the hide of an alligator.

"Um. Are you the Loch Ness Monster?" Archie stuttered, shuffling back.

"Aghhh! M—M—Monster! Monster!" Gordon turned his huge body and ran down into the cavern to hide behind a boulder no more than six feet tall in the center. His huge body was still very visible.

Archie was puzzled and looked at Jock. "Why did he do that?"

"Gordon is afraid of the M-word."

"What? *'Monster'*?" Archie whispered.

"Don't say that word around him," Jock hushed.

"Has it gone?" Gordon asked, shivering from fear.

"We can see you, Gordon. You are much bigger than the boulder. You can come out now. No need to be scared," Llewellyn said.

Gordon poked his head up over the rock, his eyes darting from side to side on the lookout for monsters. He inched back towards Archie.

"Afraid? Me? No! I'm not afraid of anything. Let me tell you something. My kind is afraid of nothing!" Gordon raised his head high.

Archie was flabbergasted at just how enormous Gordon was, when he stood tall and upright. "You are massive! Why are you so afraid of the M-word?"

Gordon's head stretched down, his long neck swinging low to Archie, his mouth just inches away. He frowned and glared. "Call me afraid again," he growled. "I just *dare* you." His hot breath warmed Archie's face.

"Calm down, Gordon. Archie never meant anything by it," Llewellyn said. "Keep that teenage temper of yours under control."

"*Teenage*?" Archie gasped.

"Yes, he's a teenager," Jock said. "Archie, how old are you?"

"I told you. I'm ten-and-a-half," Archie said indignantly.

A hushed laugh went around the cavern; the sporrans looked at each other and chuckled.

"How old are you, Gordon?" Archie asked, trying to be friendly with the huge beast before it snapped him up for a snack.

"Let me tell you, Archie. I'm two thousand six hundred and twenty-seven." Gordon paused, looking at the ceiling. "And a half."

Archie was sure Gordon was grinning at him, as the sporrans laughed some more.

"How can he be a teenager if he's over two thousand years old?" Archie asked Llewellyn.

"Sea dragons live to be sixty to seventy thousand years old." Llewellyen looked around at his fellow sporrans. "Most of us live to be a thousand years old."

"*Sea dragon*? People who have seen him think he's the Loch Ness M—" Archie stopped himself. "Well the Loch Ness M-word. They even call him Nessie."

"*Nessie*? Nessie? That's a girl's name! Who called me 'Nessie?'" Gordon snapped. "Do I look like a girl?"

"I think it's short for 'Loch Ness,'" Archie said, not wanting to say the M-word again. Archie tried pinching his own hand. Was he really talking to the Loch Ness Monster? To a sea dragon? Was he dreaming?

\*

## Chapter Seven

Llewellyn noticed Archie shivering and walked forward. "Give me your hand Archie."

Archie bent down and held Llewellyn's hand.

"You're freezing, laddie. You need to get dry and fast before you get pneumonia and end up as dead as the nuckelavee. Gordon, bend down and open wide."

"What's a nuckelavee?" Archie took a step back as Gordon's huge head came back within inches.

"Get out of those wet clothes, Archie. Hang them on Gordon's teeth."

Archie frowned, unsure if he should undress, but the warmth from Gordon's breath was welcoming. He stripped off to his underwear and hung his clothing on Gordon's teeth.

Llewellyn continued. "The nuckelavee was the most horrible of all the demons we had to fight. That was when we first moved to Scotland."

Gordon blew, and red-hot air flushed through his teeth, as Archie's clothes flapped in the hot air. Archie's face flushed as his cold body welcomed the heat. He sat down next to Llewellyn to hear more about the nuckelavee.

"Over a thousand years ago, sporrans from all over the world headed towards Scotland to seek shelter and protection from gargoyles. It was a known fact that a sea monster's scream or stare turns a gargoyle into stone. This is why on many old buildings across the lands, gargoyles peer from rooftops.

"Many of them waited, watching for sporrans to walk by, ready to swoop down and eat them. However, when Gordon was old enough, he surfaced from Loch Ness and let out a roar so loud that it could be heard from Scotland to China, from China to Australia, and on again until his mighty wail had circled the entire world. Finally, all the gargoyles were turned to stone, where they remain today.

"The nuckelavee was a horse-like demon with the teeth of a tiger and claws of a grizzly bear. It ruled the land and controlled gargoyles. It tried to kill Gordon and set all the gargoyles free from their stony postures. Gordon won with help from the sporrans, who set a trap to capture the nuckelavee. We have very fine fur, one hundred times thinner than the fur of a mink. The nuckelavee has no skin, and should the wind carry the slightest piece of our fur towards it, the nuckelavee is said to be in extreme pain, so painful it would rather be dead. So . . . it's afraid of us.

"If Gordon is killed, all the gargoyles will come back to life, along with the nuckelavee. With no sporrans left the gargoyles would turn to eat their second favorite food: human children."

Archie gulped.

"For almost a thousand years, the nuckelavee has been dead, frozen in time, and never to return. But it will try to return this year on the winter solstice.

This occurs on December 21, the shortest day of the year, at twelve minutes and twelve seconds after nine in the morning, when the moon and the sun will both appear at either side of the loch. The powerful intense light from the sun and the moon will reflect down into the loch, and legend says that this bright light can awaken the nuckelavee, who is buried down deep in the center of the loch."

Archie sat and listened carefully to everything. He wondered why he had never heard of the sporrans or the nuckelavee before. Just the sound of the creature frightened him. Although, he was sure nothing could defeat Gordon. "We should tell the police. Maybe they can get the army and kill it if it comes back."

"Oh, that is absurd!" Marlene Bardot tutted in her posh French voice. "Exactly what will you tell them? It will be something like, 'I have spoken to some sporrans, not the fake ones you hang on kilts, but real ones, and Gordon, he is what you all call 'Nessie,' he is not the Loch Ness M-word but a sea dragon. He can speak but is a little shy. Anyway, they tell me, in a few weeks' time a bigger monster called the nuckelavee is going to return and set free all the stone gargoyles, who will start eating children.'" She paused. "They will think you're insane, lock you up, and throw away the key."

Archie sat glumly listening to Marlene Bardot chastise him. "I was only trying to help."

"You tell that story and they will be giving you a triple dose of Ritalin and think you have ADHD, OCD, and probably diagnose you as NAAFC!" Marlene laughed.

"What's NAAFC?".

Marlene Bardot stood to one side with her little hand on her hip as if modeling for a magazine cover. "NAAFC stands for *'nutty as a fruit cake.'*"

The sporrans burst out laughing, and even Gordon bellowed out a deep guffaw. Archie smiled as he watched the sporrans rolling around, their little pink mouths open and eyes almost closed while they chuckled.

"Yeah I guess no one would believe me, not even my dad." Archie froze, his eyes wide open. "My dad. Oh my. What time is it? How long have I been down here?"

Archie jumped up and collected his clothes from Gordon's teeth. They were warm and dry. Suddenly, he heard a gasp from the sporrans. He slowly turned and looked at them. They were all staring at his leg. He was bleeding from two small cuts just above his ankle. Archie bent down to take a closer look. "It's okay. It doesn't hurt. I cut myself much worse than that when I fell off my bike once." Archie pulled on his clothing.

"Oh dear," Jock said as he walked closer to inspect Archie's cuts. He paused and looked at Gordon.

Gordon looked away. "Let me tell you something: I had to grip him tight. He was drowning and looked so sad moments before he fell in. I had to save him!"

"It's fine. It doesn't even hurt. Well, maybe burns a bit. That's all." Archie's remark brought another gasp from the sporrans. "Gordon saved my life, and he couldn't help it. I was fighting and kicking."

"I'm sorry, Archie. Forgive me," Gordon said gloomily.

"Consider yourself forgiven." Archie smiled and imitated Gordon. "Let me tell you something. I am pleased you saved me." The sporrans chuckled at how deep Archie's voice was. Archie looked up at the ceiling. "What are the lights in the ceiling of the cavern?"

Gordon and the sporrans looked up at the tiny bright lights that covered the ceiling and walls. At first, Archie had mistaken them for thousands of stars twinkling.

Jock explained they were crystallized fireflies that had died thousands of years ago after being trapped. Water from above had seeped through the rock face, and the lime and minerals in the water had crystallized them. They lit the whole cavern up like Christmas trees lights. Huge stalactites and stalagmites grew from the ceiling and the ground. The cavern was massive and seemed to go on deep underground.

## Chapter Eight

Archie had a question and was almost afraid to ask it. Eventually he got the courage. "If the fireflies couldn't get out, does that mean we can't?"

"We can get out. Miner makes tunnels for us, because that's how we eat." Jock explained that sporrans live on a healthy diet of potatoes and carrots. Miner tunnels his way to the surface, under most local farms and gardens. Some humans think they have a mole problem when they notice the yard or lawn dug up. If he finds any area where he can collect potatoes or where carrots grow, he will hang around for a week or more. Sometimes he may pop up in someone's yard only to discover an apple tree, black currant bush, or even strawberries a few houses away. All make up the diet of the sporrans.

Archie looked around at the sporrans. Many sat around the floor and watched Archie, fascinated by him. Many had never seen a human up close before. Naturally they were scared of him. After all, they had heard the stories regarding humans eating haggis and hanging dead sporrans around their waists. Archie, on the other hand, was friendly and seemed harmless.

"Which one of you is Miner?" Archie asked.

Marlene Bardot tutted. "Typical English boy. Not very bright. The French boys are much smarter. Surely you can spot that *dégueulasse* sporran?"

"Day goo what?"

"*Dégueulasse*. It's French and means dirty, disgusting, crude, and nasty. Or in other words: Miner." Marlene sneered with her little pink hand on her hip.

"I love it when you talk dirty, Marlene," said a gruff-sounding voice. From the scurry of sporrans came what first Archie thought was a brown sporran, but on closer inspection, the sporran was just covered in mud. He wore a little hat made from a rusty sardine tin, and on front of that, he had a lump of stone with crystallized fireflies. It made a perfect miner's lamp.

Archie laughed when he saw him. "You must be Miner. It's a pleasure to meet you, sir."

Miner Sporran paced towards Archie and held out his little pink hand and shook Archie's hand. Miner took a step back and dusted himself off, and a large cloud of brown dust smothered the other sporrans, who started to complain and cough.

*

Alec arrived home to discover an empty house. After a half hour of looking for him, he called Chloe's parents. She had not seen him since they said goodbye at the boat garage. Alec called Foyers Police, and most of the village helped in the search. Jack and Peggy Macdonald asked the regulars at the pub to join in the search. Two local fishermen took out a small boat and started to search the side of the Loch just in case Archie had fallen in.

When the police arrived Alec was pacing up and down outside his home. He chastised himself for not having walked Archie home. A ten-year-old boy wasn't old enough to go home on his own, even though it was just a few hundred yards, he thought to himself.

Peggy did her best to reassure Alec that Archie would be fine. "He's probably just gone exploring. You know what boys are like at that age. He will turn up and wonder what all the fuss is about."

"Can the lad swim, Alec?" Jack asked.

"Yes, I think so. He had a ten-meter certificate for swimming." Alec knew that swimming ten meters in a heated swimming pool was not the same as trying to swim in the loch, especially in November when the water was icy cold.

The evening darkness covered the village. A helicopter flew in from Inverness to search the area. The huge spotlight concentrated mainly on the loch. They assumed the boy had gotten too close to the edge and had fallen in.

"Some kind of dad I turned out to be. I only had the boy a few days and I've already lost him," Alec said, fighting back tears.

Peggy put her arm around him trying to comfort him. A few of the volunteers started to wander back. The icy cold air was taking its toll. Many knew a small boy wouldn't survive much longer out in the cold, and if he had fallen in the water, he probably got hyperthermia in five minutes.

*

Archie looked at Miner's lamp. "That's wicked and you'll never need a battery. Is there a tunnel that goes to the surface? I had better get back home. I think my dad will be worried."

"Yes, there are tunnels everywhere. I can travel under most of Scotland. But I dig them for me. You're much too large. You'd never fit in my tunnels."

Archie looked desolate and had to stop himself from crying. Anxiously, he asked Gordon, "Can you help me get home?"

Gordon nodded. He bowed his huge head close down to Archie. "Let me tell you something. There is a way, but it's very dangerous."

"I'll do it. I can't stay down here forever."

"No, it's too dangerous, Gordon." Jock walked forward and put himself between Archie and Gordon.

Archie gently brushed Jock's fluffy white head. "I will be okay if I'm with Gordon."

Gordon coughed. "That is the problem, Archie. You could squeeze in my mouth. I could take you back to the surface and spit you out."

"Okay that'll work. What's so dangerous about that?"

"Well my main diet is fish, the occasional duck, and, if I'm lucky, a sheep or cow that gets too close to the bank of the loch." Gordon inhaled through his nose, sniffing Archie's aroma. "You smell quite tasty. Once you are in my mouth and I get into the water, millions of years of natural evolution and sea dragon instinct might take over and you could end up as a tasty snack."

Archie's eyes widened. He took two steps back, almost stepping on Miner Sporran.

## Chapter Nine

Archie said goodbye to the sporrans. Jock hugged Archie's leg, as he stood just below Archie's knee. "I'm gonna miss you, Archie. I've never met a human before."

Gordon lowered his bottom jaw on the ground and opened his mouth. Archie nervously climbed over the razor-sharp teeth. Gordon gave a deep, hoarse growl from deep inside when Archie stepped onto his tongue. The sound frightened Archie.

"Oops. Sorry," Archie said.

Gordon's mouth gently closed, and Archie sat in total darkness. Gordon felt cold to the touch, like raw meat, his breath hot and steamy. He held on tight as Gordon lifted his head, reminding Archie of being in an elevator or on a ride at the fairground.

The sea dragon walked into the water in the underground lake and was soon consumed by the loch's icy waters. His powerful tail kicked and forced him down to the hidden entrance. It was a journey Gordon had taken for over a thousand years, although never with a warm, living mammal in his mouth. He flicked his tail to the side with a powerful stroke, propelling him into the loch. He swam upwards at great speed, and as he approached the surface, he slowed and watched from a few feet below.

When Gordon thought it was safe, he moved within a few feet of the bank and spat Archie out. Archie was expecting to be dropped off on the bank, not unceremoniously spat out into the water. He gasped in shock from the cold water and started kicking. Gordon came up behind him and nudged him to the side. Archie caught the rock face and pulled himself out onto the bank, gasping for air. Mr. MacGregor heard the splashing. He was nearby smoking a pipe, and he aimed his flashlight and spotted Archie climbing out of the loch.

"Are you okay, laddie?" The scary old man with the bushy sideburns reached out with his *shillelagh*. "You must be Archie Wilson. The villagers have been looking for you. Catch the end of my *shillelagh*."

Archie took hold of the end of the *shillelagh*, and Mr. MacGregor pulled him to his feet. Archie, shivering, turned and looked into the loch. Gordon was gone. Archie wondered if he would ever see him or the sporrans again.

"I've found him!" Mr. MacGregor shouted. "I've found the boy!"

Within minutes, a crowd gathered, followed by the police and an ambulance. Mr. MacGregor disappeared into the crowd. Archie was taken to Inverness Hospital in an ambulance with Alec for fear he had pneumonia .

"I can't believe you're alive, son. That water is icy this time of the year. How long were you in the water?" Alec asked.

"I went for walk and fell in. I don't think I was in there for too long."

"It was several hours, and by all accounts, you should be dead."

Archie closed his eyes and feigned sleep. In the short time he had known his father, Archie had come to like him. He was doing his best to make Archie feel wanted and accepted. Archie didn't relish the idea of lying to his father. He thought it better to ignore the questions for now, and maybe later, they would stop asking.

The doctors at Inverness County Hospital were flummoxed by his condition. His temperature was high, not dangerously so, but much higher than they would have expected for someone who fell in the loch. Then there was his heartbeat—slow and relaxed. His vital signs were perfect, and he was given a clean bill of health. If anything, they said he was extremely healthy.

That's when Archie first noticed it. When he was getting dressed into some dry clothes his father had brought him, the cuts he had earlier from Gordon's teeth had completely healed. There wasn't a scratch on him, yet Archie was certain that, earlier, he had been bleeding so badly the sporrans had gasped. Maybe he had dreamed the whole thing?

He looked at his father. "I lost my glasses. Sorry."

"We can go to the opticians tomorrow. Will you be okay until then?"

"Yeah, I seem to be okay for now."

Archie was later introduced to Jack and Peggy MacDonald at the White Stag Inn. Peggy was in her late sixties. She had grey curly hair and a friendly round face with a large mole on her cheek. She made a fuss of Archie and explained to him how worried his father had been. And under no circumstances was Archie to wander off again.

Normally children under fourteen were not allowed in the bar when it was open, but tonight they made an exception for Archie. He sat in front of the massive fireplace watching the logs hiss and spit flames up the chimney. Above the fireplace was a framed black and white picture of what was reported to be the Loch Ness Monster. Archie gazed up at it and didn't think it looked anything like Gordon. His father came and sat next to him, unsure whether or not to put his arm around the young boy. They weren't yet that close, so he settled for rubbing Archie's knee. He followed Archie's eyes to the picture. "That'll be Nessie. The Loch Ness Monster."

"Nessie is a girl's name," Archie said.

"Aye, it is that," old Jack Macdonald said, emptying his pipe by tapping it against the brick. "Legend has it that Nessie is neither male or female. It lives in the loch and can live for thousands of years. When it's time comes to pass away, it will lay an egg. That egg won't hatch until the old sea monster has died."

Archie watched Mr. Macdonald fill his pipe with tobacco. "At school, they said if you smoke you get thick black tar in your lungs. Mr. Macdonald, it's not good for you."

Mr. Macdonald smiled and lit his pipe. "Is that so?" He blew out a puff of smoke. "Good, that tar will keep me warm in the winter months."

Archie opened his mouth to reply, but nothing came out. His face looked pained as he tried to come up with a reply. His father shook his head and nodded. Archie was unsure whose side he was on and thought it best not to mention it again.

The heat was warm to Archie's face. He leaned against his father listening to stories about Nessie and eventually fell asleep.

\*

"Archie. Come, laddie, it's time to get up," Alec said, shaking his son. Archie opened his eyes. It took him a second or two to wake. "Come on downstairs now. I have hot tea and porridge for you."

Archie nodded and took in his surroundings. He was in bed, dressed in his pajamas. The last thing he remembered was sitting in front of the fire at the pub. He jumped from his bed and looked out his window. Coils of mist-like translucent silk mixed with delicate rain were rolling down the mountains on either side of the loch. The water was calm. He wondered if he had dreamed the whole underwater cavern experience. Was it real? Had he met a talking sea dragon named Gordon and actually made friends with sporrans?

On his way to the bathroom, Archie stopped outside his father's room. The door was open, and inside, so was the wardrobe door. Hanging on a coat hanger was his father's kilt, dark red with a green pattern. Archie guessed it was the McIntosh tartan. But what really caught his attention was the white furry sporran hanging from the center.

Archie tiptoed in and felt it. "Hello," Archie whispered, examining it. The sporran had no hands or feet, and if it had any eyes or a mouth, they were closed. On the top was an opening. Archie peered inside; it was lined with cotton. Inside a label: Morrison Sporran Manufactures. The top had a silver clasp, just like a purse. He felt the fur, real fur, but it felt more like wool and was cold. It was nothing like little Jock Sporran.

# Chapter Ten

When he returned to school, Archie had achieved an unwanted celebrity status. Overnight, everyone knew who Archie Wilson was. He was the boy who went missing, feared lost and turned up soaking wet climbing out of the loch.

Like most ten-year-olds, Archie settled in fairly quickly to his new school. Chloe mentioned she went to Inverness on Friday nights to swim. They had a swimming club for ages eight to fourteen, and she asked Archie if he wanted to go. He said he would ask his father.

The school day seemed to fly by. Archie was met at the gate by his father, and together they travelled to Inverness to see an optician to replace the glasses he'd lost.

The optician, Dr. Huey McPhee, was a tall, thin man with greying red hair. He was rather rude to most people, but always friendly to children. McPhee Opticians had been in Inverness for over sixty years. Archie was shown into his office with his father.

"So, Archie, you lost your glasses and I suppose you have no idea of your subscription?" Dr. McPhee asked.

"No, sir. My mom did all that stuff." Archie shrugged sadly.

"Not a problem, I would want to check them again anyway." Huey pointed at a Snellen chart on the wall. "Let's start from the top, Archie. With both eyes, work your way down as far as you can."

Archie looked at the sign and started. "E, F, P, T, O, Z." He kept going—the second line, third, fourth, fifth, sixth. By the time he got to the tenth, Dr. McPhee and Alec looked at each other in wonder. Archie kept going and read line eleven and continued. "Printed by Watkins and Son Limited."

The room fell silent before Dr. McPhee eventually broke the silence. "Is this some kind of a joke?" he asked Alec.

"He was wearing glasses when I picked him up in London. His eyes are better than mine. I can't read below line eight!" Alec said.

"Did I do okay?" Archie asked.

"You don't need glasses, Archie, your eyes are . . . Well, some people with good eyesight have twenty-twenty vision, but you, my dear boy, seem to have twenty-ten vision or higher."

"Oh, is that bad?" Archie said glumly.

"No, dear boy, that's almost as good as a hawk. Why ever did you wear glasses?" Dr. McPhee asked, looking into Archie's eyes with a small flashlight. "I've never, in all my days, seen someone read all eleven lines and finish off with the small print at the bottom. I didn't even know it was there."

"I couldn't see very well without them. I don't miss them. I think I can see just as good now as I did with them. Well, maybe better. They told me if I wore my glasses, my eyes would improve. I thought they were just saying that to make me wear them."

Dr. McPhee studied the boy. "Aye. We do say that to smaller children, but rarely will your eyes improve so much you don't need glasses. As for you . . . Well, you don't need any. That's for sure."

Archie was excited when he was told he didn't need glasses again. On the journey home, it struck him that everything was clearer; he could read signs that were way ahead in the distance.

Archie noticed a few other changes over the next few days.. He knocked a pen off the table and caught it before it hit the floor and he longer felt the cold weather. When outside. He put it down to growing up and getting older.

He found it rather weird yet wonderful having a girl as a friend. Then again, Chloe was no ordinary girl. She could climb a tree as good as any boy her age. She was just as fast on her bicycle as the boys and didn't seem to be scared of anything. She even picked up a worm that had wriggled its way onto the school playground and placed it on the side where the asphalt joined the grass. Much to the disgust of many other girls and even some boys, she carried it in her hand, talking to it as if it were a pet hamster.

Archie still found her Scottish accent hard to understand, especially if she got excited and talked fast. She was nothing like Archie's old friend Imran, but she made him laugh just as much and wasn't afraid to use the odd curse word.

Every morning she waited outside the school for him. Her blue eyes glistened and round chubby, freckle-covered cheeks glowed as she smiled. He enjoyed her company and looked forward to seeing her and going swimming with her. She had told him she had already got her twenty-five-meter swimming badge and was hoping to get a hundred-meter badge soon.

\*

Chloe's dad, Mr. Stewart, spoke to Alec just before they left for swimming. Archie thought they seemed to know each other quite well but didn't seem very close. Then again, everyone in Foyers knew everyone else *and* everyone else's business. Chloe told Archie if you farted in the library the whole village would know about it within a day. That was the disadvantage of living in a small Scottish village. Not that doing that kind of thing in a library is a good thing. But when you are ten years old and someone passes wind, it is very funny indeed.

Archie later found out that his dad disliked the company Mr. Stewart worked for, the Green Oil Company. His father told him that just because they had the word "green" in the company name didn't mean the company was environmentally good. In fact, they had a reputation of destroying the countryside by installing oil pipes and causing pollution.

Archie sat in the back of the car next to Chloe. Evan, her older brother, sat in the front passenger seat. He turned and looked at Archie. "So you're the great *Archie Wilson* that we were searching for last week. The boy who Chloe talks about all the time." Evan looked Archie up and down.

"I don't talk about him all the time." Chloe blushed. "Take no notice of him Archie. Evan is the smelliest person in the whole of Scotland, and he's as blind as a bat."

"I'm not blind, you little Numpty," Evan snapped back. Archie had to hide his smirk when he heard the nickname Evan had for his little sister.

"You *are* blind. How come when you go to the bathroom you get pee all over the floor? You are either blind or your widget is that small you can't aim it."

Archie roared with laughter but stopped when he noticed Evan glaring at him. The last thing Archie wanted was to be thumped by a thirteen-year-old.

Chloe and Evan's dad, Mr. Stewart, embarrassed his children by trying to sing along to tunes on the radio. Archie liked him because he reminded him of his own father, and although he had just recently met his own father, he had already come to like him. But he missed his mom more each day. He was worried he would forget what she looked like, the sound of her voice, her gentle kiss on his forehead, and her scent.

Evan took Archie to the boys' changing rooms. He showed Archie the lockers, and as soon as he saw his own friends, he left Archie alone to find his own way to the pool.

As a new boy, Archie was put in the same group as Chloe, and he was pleasantly surprised at the warmth of the pool. It was an Olympic-size pool, larger than the pool he went to in London. At one end, it had an extra pool that was over twenty feet deep with diving platforms so high Archie thought he could possibly touch the ceiling from the highest one.

"Can you swim a length yet, Archie?" Angus, the instructor, asked.

"No, sir. I have my ten-meter badge," Archie said proudly.

"Well, go to the top of the pool and wait for the instructor in the red tracksuit to tell you what to do," Angus barked.

"What? The deep end?" Archie gulped.

Angus just pointed and turned to talk to another swimmer.

Archie walked towards the deep end. The water seemed a darker blue color as he got to the end. The instructor in the red tracksuit barked orders at swimmers going up and down the pool. Evan and his friends swam lengths in different strokes and styles.

The instructor told Archie to climb in and hold onto the side. He picked up what Archie could only describe as a broomstick and held it by Archie's head. "Now, Archie I want you to swim to the other end of the pool. If you get tired, grab the side or my stick, and I will walk alongside."

"How far?" Archie asked looking down to the other end of the pool. "I can only swim ten meters."

"No, Archie. You have only swam ten meters. You can swim as far as you want or until you struggle. Now off you go."

Archie took a deep breath, reluctantly pushed off from the end, and swam parallel with the side. He was pleased to see the instructor walking alongside, keeping the stick just a few inches away from Archie's grasp should he need it.

"Lift your legs higher," the instructor said. "Stretch your arms further, and kick harder, Archie."

Following the instructions, Archie kept going and going and going. He passed the half-way mark, twenty-five meters, and kept going. Angus noticed Archie and the instructor coming towards them. He stopped what he was doing and watched.

Farther and farther, Archie swam as the end was getting closer. Archie's fingers touched the end of the pool. He stopped and stood up. He had made it all the way to the shallow end: fifty meters.

"You told me you could only swim ten meters," Angus smiled. "You just swam fifty."

Archie looked wide-eyed at both instructors. "Can I go back up?"

Before the night was over Archie had swam a hundred meters and was given his new badge and certificate. He was slightly disappointed to find out he would not be getting a twenty-five-meter badge, but overjoyed he had a hundred-meter certificate.

Driving back to Foyers, Archie held his one-hundred-meter certificate in one hand and cloth badge in the other.

He wondered if his dad knew how to sew. He still had his ten-meter badge and wanted both sewn onto his coat to wear to swimming club. He noticed Evan didn't have any on his coat and couldn't remember seeing any others wearing them. Maybe they didn't sew on swimming badges in Scotland. As the car travelled through Foyers, Archie was in such deep though he never noticed the police car outside the church.

"Hey, Archie. The police are here. They've come to arrest you for lying about your swimming," Evan joked.

Archie looked up. A police car was parked outside the church with two police officers talking to local people. He felt sick, dizzy, and shaken.

"Archie didn't lie about anything," Chloe snapped back.

"He said he could only swim ten meters. It was pretty obvious he can swim further than that. I bet he swam that far before and just wanted a badge and certificate."

"No, I've never swam that far before," Archie said, his voice trailing off as he watched the police. Mr. Stewart stopped the car and climbed out. He spoke to some of the locals, who were pointing up at the church roof. After a few minutes he climbed back into the car. "They say someone stole the gargoyles from the church roof. Those things must have weighed a ton."

"Why would they steal those ugly things?" Evan asked.

"Some rich guy probably wants them around his fancy fish pond. Many of the old large Scottish homes are being bought by rich southerners. They buy them and fix them up, thinking they are lords of the manor," Mr. Stewart said.

"Stupid English," Evan said, making sure Archie could hear.

Archie sat back again. He was relieved it was not bad news. But what if the gargoyles had come back to life? What if the nuckelavee had come back and broke Gordon's spell?

*

Archie sat in front of the fire, drinking a hot mug of chocolate and eating oatmeal-raisin cookies with his dad. His father had placed Archie's new certificate in a frame. Archie held the mug in both hands and sipped the delicious drink. He sat pondering, watching the flames dance in the fireplace.

"Dad," Archie asked quietly. "Have you ever heard of the nuckelavee?" It was the first time he called him "Dad." Once he had said it, he thought it sounded natural.

Alec smiled and almost got teary-eyed hearing Archie call him "Dad." "Who or what put that thought in your head, son? But since you asked . . . the nuckelavee is an old folk tale. A myth. Not real. Just like the Loch Ness Monster. 'Nuckelavee' means devil of the sea.

"The nuckelavee is the worst of all demons. Its sole purpose is to plague the local people. It is said to have a skinless head of a horse and the feet of a lion. Its breath is venom and can give all our crops fungus and disease. It spreads pure evil. Some say it sits on the back of the horse-like creature. The head and body is part-man, part-rat. Its body joins the body of the creature it rides. The head has one eye, and that eye can stop a man's heart with a single stare."

Archie nervously shifted closer to his father. "Has anyone seen it?"

"No, and don't be having nightmares. It's just an old myth. But you asked so I told you." Alec rubbed Archie's head. He got up and turned the TV on. "I want to see the football results. Celtic was playing the Rangers tonight." He switched the channel to BBC. The news was showing an image of the prime minister who was discussing mortgage interest rates, something Archie found boring. He yawned and sipped his hot chocolate.

The next news article caught Archie's attention, though. At London's Westminster Cathedral, someone had stolen two of the gargoyles from the roof, and the thieves had also targeted a few other churches and buildings across the country.

# Chapter Eleven

That same night, four hundred miles away in Coventry, England, twin fourteen-year-old brothers Bryan and Billy Butcher broke into Coventry Cathedral. It was just past midnight, so they were sure no one would be around. It was the perfect crime, Bryan told his brother.

They had seen the same news on TV and suspected that various gangs of thieves had been stealing gargoyles. They knew the cathedral as well as anyone. They had both attended Sunday school and been in the cathedral choir. That was just over two years ago. Life was different now. Their father once had a job at the local car plant on the assembly line that produced the Rover car. Since it closed two years ago, their father had not worked. He had taken to drink and constantly fought with their mother, who held two jobs trying to make ends meet.

Bryan and Billy had pretty much been left to fend for themselves. Often, they skipped school and hung around in derelict buildings with older kids, many of them school drop-outs from the same housing estate.

Although Bryan was a few minutes younger than Billy, he always did the thinking for the pair. Billy followed him and did whatever his brother suggested. Tonight's get-rich-quick plan was simple. They'd steal a box cart from a neighbor and drag it to the Cathedral. They would break in, climb the stairs to the bell tower, and use the maintenance door to access the roof. From the rooftop, they'd remove a gargoyle and lower it down to the ground by a rope they'd stolen from a building site.

Rather than risk trying to sell the gargoyle, Bryan had an ingenious plan: they would take pictures of it once they had it secured and hidden in their grandfather's shed. They'd send the pictures and a ransom note for two hundred pounds to the archbishop. Bryan was sure the archbishop would pay up. After all, the church was extremely wealthy.

The gruesome-looking gargoyle was on the edge of the building, as if about to jump on passersby below. "Wow! It's freezing up here," Billy complained as the icy wind blew through his spiky, gelled hair. "Why are we taking this one? It looks older and nasty and it may not be worth as much."

"If it's older it could be an antique and worth more. You'll soon warm up when we lower the gargoyle down to the ground. It looks heavy." Bryan tied a rope around the waist of the gargoyle. Once it was secured, he passed the rope to Billy. "Hold it tight as soon as I break off the cement. It will fall and we don't want to damage it, else we can say goodbye to our two hundred quid."

Bryan started smashing the base of the gargoyle with the hammer working his way around.

"Stop," Billy hissed.

Bryan paused and looked at his brother. "What?"

"I thought it moved." Billy stared at the gargoyle.

"Of course it did, it's coming free. A few more whacks, and it will be loose. Now, hold on tight to the rope."

"No, I thought *it* actually moved, like its head moved. Must be the wind." He narrowed his eyes, studying the gargoyle.

Billy positioned himself back from the edge. He sat on the roof and dug his heels into a ridge, getting ready to take the weight. Bryan gave a few more heavy blows with the hammer, and the cement holding the feet of the gargoyle gave. The gargoyle plummeted. It weighed over two hundred pounds, more that the two fourteen-year olds' weight combined.

Billy yelped in pain as the rope burnt his hands. "I can't hold it. It's too heavy!"

Bryan joined him and caught hold of the rope. With both of them holding the rope, they were able to stop its rapid decent.

"This thing weighs a ton," Billy complained. "It's giving me rope burns on my fingers."

It was nearly two hundred feet to the ground below. The weight was getting too much for the boys. The rope was blistering and burning their hands, the pain unbearable.

"Thanks, that's better," Billy said, noticing it was getting lighter.

"Nuh-uh! It's not me. It must be stuck on something. It's getting lighter."

They were up on the roof and back from the edge and couldn't see the gargoyle. Eventually, it went completely light.

"Uh oh. I think the rope broke, or it came untied. Get ready for the crash," Bryan said.

The rope went completely slack. They waited a few moments to hear the expected crash, but no sound came. Just silence. Side by side, they crawled to the edge of the roof. As they both peered over the edge, they had the shock of their young lives.

Just inches from them was the gargoyle, its wings flapping, flying right in front of them. The grotesque creature's breath smelled like nothing they had smelled before. It was a horrid smell, from somewhere deep down in the sewer of the planet. The hideous head was covered in pus seeping from scabs, and a swarm of large black flies circled it.

Its head turned slowly and faced them, its red eyes glinting, its mouth spread from one side of its face to the other. The mouth showed its decaying teeth and purple tongue. It had been over a thousand years since its last meal. The two young brothers must have looked appetizing. They froze, too scared to scream or cry for help.

Twenty-four hours later, Bryan and Billy Butcher's mother filed two missing person reports with the local police. Despite searches the teenage boys were never seen again.

\*

Like most boys his age, Archie didn't pay attention to the news. It was boring and usually about politics, a war, or a tragic story on poor, starving people in a country he had never heard of. More often were stories about an old celebrity who passed away. It was different now, though. Archie heard more and more stories about the gargoyles being stolen. He wondered if there was more to the story than was being reported.

He thought about telling Chloe, but he liked her and she might think he was crazy. How could he tell her he had met the Loch Ness Monster and had even taken a ride in its mouth? For now, he kept his thoughts to himself. A week passed and more reports came on the news.

\*

Sunday. The weather turned dry but rather windy. After eating lunch, a knock came at the door. Chloe was there, carrying a kite. Archie later found out that whenever it was dry and windy, Chloe and Evan liked to fly kites above the loch.

"Hold the kite still. You don't have to run. When I say, just let go," Chloe ordered. She was wearing a knitted pink hat with matching scarf, red rubber boots that came just below her knees, and a purple padded coat. "Go!"

Archie let go and immediately the kite took to the sky. Chloe called it a stunt kite. Evan called his a more sophisticated name: a dual-line kite. They looked the same to Archie. Both had two strings so they could maneuver the kite up in the sky and turn it to the left or right. Evan's kite was black with two menacing-looking eyes, while Chloe's was orange and had the face of a cat.

They flew the kites in circles like experts. The kites swooped low to the loch, almost touching the water's surface and then raced back up into the sky again. Archie watched, fascinated, as Chloe and Evan gasped and sighed and squatted and twisted, maneuvering the kites in ways that seemed beyond the rules of physics.

"Come here, Archie. You can have a go!" Chloe smiled.

Of course, Archie wanted to try, but he was a little apprehensive. He didn't want to crash it into the loch. Chloe raised her arms and brought them down either side of his body. She moved close to his back, her arms stretched, and told him to hold her wrists. Having never been this close to a girl before, Archie felt a little awkward. She explained if he pushed his right hand forward and pulled back on the left, the kite would descend to the left and vice versa.

"Take the spools and don't let them go," Chloe instructed.

Immediately, Archie could feel the sheer power of the wind. Chloe held his wrists and showed him how to control the kite. He found it exhilarating, having control of an object that could soar high into the sky in one movement and, in the next, could fly in a figure eight or spin down to the surface and up again. Evan was more adventurous with his, allowing the tail of the kite to touch the water.

That night, Archie asked his father for a kite. He needed one more than anything else in the world. He was told, with Christmas just a few weeks away, maybe Santa would bring him one. A few weeks seemed like a lifetime.

While Archie was surprised how much he enjoyed living in Foyers with his father, not a day went by without thoughts of his mother. Sometimes, if he and Chloe were laughing at something, he would feel guilty. *Should I be sad? Is it wrong for me to laugh?* he asked himself. He consoled himself remembering what she had always told him when he had had an argument with a friend over something petty: "Friends come and go, but life goes on, and around each corner is a new friend." Her clever words meant more now and seemed to have come true, for despite his broken heart for his mother, he had now found his dad and some new best friends.

## Chapter Twelve

Deborah Reynolds woefully pushed her three-month-old son Clint in the stroller. It was a two-mile walk she had taken the last nine weeks. She stopped at the same shop to buy a bouquet of flowers. Yellow today, they were bright and cheerful because she needed cheering up. Even after five months, she was just as depressed today as she was *that day* the casualty assistance officer from the Royal Marines knocked at her door. When he informed her that her husband Clint had died in action in Afghanistan, her hopes and dreams were shattered. When the bad news finally sunk in, the grief was unbearable, and she struggled to accept it. She cried for days, saying life was unfair. They were expecting a baby. Clint would never see his son. And her soon-to-be-born child would never meet his father.

Each week, Deborah pushed her son baby Clint Jr. to the small Oxford Church and made her way among the gravestones. She applied the brake on the stroller at the graveside. Lovingly, she brushed away the fallen autumn leaves and wiped the headstone clean. A tear ran down her cheek as she read. *Clint Reynolds. 1990-2015. Beloved husband of Deborah. Rest in Peace.*

Baby Clint Jr. was cooing and gurgling, and his little hands were covered in blue, knit mittens. He wriggled his arms and watched his mittens wave in front of his face.

Deborah knelt down next to the grave and placed the new yellow flowers in the vase. It was a cloudy day. If it had been sunny then maybe she would have seen the large shadow as it flew over her.

After a few minutes talking to the headstone and updating her late husband on his son's progress, she stopped. Baby Clint Jr. was making no noise. Deborah climbed to her feet and checked the stroller. To her horror, it was empty. No one was around. The graveyard was deserted. She screamed and frantically ran to the church, but it was locked. Tears streamed down her face, as she looked out into the street. Did someone take baby Clint Jr.?

She ran back to the stroller and checked again. Empty. Hysterical, Deborah ran out of the graveyard and into the street screaming for her son. She turned, but it was too late. The van skidded at the last second but had no time to stop. Deborah was knocked several feet up into the air and was thrown into an oncoming car and, eventually, onto her back in the middle of the street.

Unfamiliar faces looked down at her. Her
head felt heavy and throbbed with pain. Her
stomach was in severe agony. A woman knelt
down and spoke to her. That's when Deborah
saw it. Over the woman's shoulder. Something
dark moved on top of the church. Her vision
was blurry, so she couldn't quite make it out.
Then she saw something else. This time, a blue
mitten floating down from the church roof. She
opened her mouth to tell someone. She wanted
to scream out and ask for help. No sound came
from her mouth. She was gone.

*

Archie went swimming again on Friday
with Chloe and Evan. He swam several lengths
of the pool with ease. When the swimming
lessons were over, they were allowed fifteen
minutes free time. They enjoyed free time
because they could do whatever they wanted,
like bombing each other. Others played tag in
the water.

He watched Evan and some of the more experienced swimmers attempting to swim a full length under water. Evan made it three-quarters of the length of the pool. His friend Thomas not only made it to the end and turned around underwater but managed to swim back a few feet. Applause met him when he surfaced and gasped for air.

Archie had never swum underwater before but would try it anyway. When it was his turn, he clumsily dived in and started swimming under the water. He opened his eyes. At first, they stung, but he quickly adjusted. He found it easier than he thought, so he continued to swim along the bottom of the pool, avoiding some of the other swimmers' legs and kicking feet.

He made it to the end of the pool faster than he had expected. He turned underwater just like he had observed Thomas do earlier. Archie pushed off from the wall keeping his chest just inches from the bottom. He continued until he made it all the way back up to the deep end, eventually touching the wall. When he surfaced, he couldn't quite believe it. He had just swum two lengths of the pool underwater. He held onto the side and looked around. Feeling slightly disappointed that no one had noticed, he climbed out.

He was quiet on the way home. He thanked Chloe and her father for taking him and thought about telling his dad. He was dropped off at the White Stag. His father was working tonight behind the bar. The MacDonalds made Archie a room up when his father worked in the bar. From the room just above the bar, he could hear the occasional laugh and constant chatter from the customers. His room was small but clean, and Peggy MacDonald had bought a set of sheets and matching Spider-Man bed cover. She also placed a bedside lamp with matching Spider-Man lampshade. Spider-Man wasn't a character Archie particularly followed, but he appreciated the gesture. They had also put a small TV in the room for him.

The MacDonalds had made Archie's arrival to Scotland much easier. It soon became clear to Archie that his father had no idea how to look after children, what they liked to do or eat, or what a ten-year-old could or could not do for himself. Archie made his own bed in the mornings but couldn't make his own dinner. When he took a bath, his mother had washed his hair, but his father didn't seem sure what to do and always knocked before entering the bathroom. Archie appreciated his father trying his best. He knew if his father had not taken him, he might have ended up in an orphanage or with foster parents. As it turned out, he was happy to be living with his real father in Foyers. The Macdonalds were like grandparents.

With a cup of hot chocolate and some cookies in hand, he turned on the TV and flipped through the channels. The news came on with a picture of a stone gargoyle. The reporter mentioned more had gone missing from the roof of a church. The next item on the news was a sad story of a woman in Oxford getting run over by a van. Police were mystified why she had run into the busy street. They had been unable to find her baby and were appealing to the public for information. Archie's heart started to race, his stomach tying itself up in knots. The picture changed to a scene at the accident. A news reporter holding a microphone with the letters BBC on it spoke to the camera. Archie's attention was drawn to the church roof in the background. The reporter named the church as Oxford Holy Trinity Church. Archie noticed there were no gargoyles on the rooftop.

He put his chocolate down and crept into the next room the MacDonalds used as an office. It had a desk buried under papers and a computer with a massive thick monitor like an old TV from the movies.

"Please don't have a password," Archie whispered to himself as he pressed the power button. The computer whirled to life. It seemed to be slower than the ones they used at school or the computer his mom used to have. Eventually he figured how to get onto the Internet and searched "Oxford Trinity Church." Within seconds, he had hit the image tag, and after a scroll down the page, Archie almost froze.

Sure enough, on all the images of the church he could see gargoyles on the roof. Yet today, on the news, no gargoyles. And a baby was missing. The thought made Archie sick. The sporrans had told him about this. If he had told someone, the Oxford lady may still be alive, and her baby would not be missing or worse.

Archie heard footsteps coming up the stairs. He powered the computer off and ran back to his room.

"You should be in bed, Archie." Peggy Macdonald smiled. "It's past nine o'clock."

"I don't have school tomorrow," Archie said, sipping his chocolate.

"I don't care, laddie. It's late. Now put your pajamas on and get into bed. I'll be up later to check on you."

"Mrs. Macdonald, have you heard about the gargoyles that have gone missing?"

"Aye, I have. Probably kids. Now it's a craze all over the country."

"Do you think they could come back to life?"

"No! That's nonsense. But if they do, you can be sure they will be on the lookout for ten-year-old boys who stay up too late. Now, get to bed. We're busy tonight. Your dad is working hard. I don't know what we'd do without him." Peggy closed the door.

When he finally climbed into bed, he had trouble sleeping. His head was full of questions. Had the gargoyles come to life? Was the nuckelavee summoning all the gargoyles? Were the gargoyles responsible for the missing baby? A few cats had gone missing too, was that the work of the gargoyles? *How come I could swim so far under water?*

## Chapter Thirteen

After a large cooked breakfast at the White Stag Inn with Peggy, Archie walked home. There, he found his dad at the kitchen reading the paper and drinking tea.

"Morning, Archie. Did you sleep well? Did you have breakfast yet?"

"Yes, I slept fine and had eggs and bacon for breakfast. Mrs. Macdonald is really nice."

"They're good people. I couldn't live on what I make from the boat yard. We don't have the tourists here like we used to, so there aren't so many boats that need repairing. We need Nessie to show his face again."

"You mean Gordon," Archie said without thinking.

"Who's Gordon?"

"Um . . . well, we don't know the Loch Ness Monster is called Nessie. He might be called Gordon. Nessie is a girl's name," Archie stuttered.

"Well, Nessie might *be* a girl."

*If Gordon heard you say that he would roast you alive,* Archie thought.

"Dad, can I call Imran today and later go and see Chloe?" Archie asked. Even though he had been with his father for two weeks he still found it strange calling him "Dad."

"Sure. I'm pleased you made new friends."

*

Imran was excited to hear from Archie. He wanted to know when he was coming back to London. The main purpose of the phone call was to tell Imran about the gargoyles and Gordon, but once they started talking, Archie never mentioned it. Imran seemed to be part of his past life, and he remembered he had promised the sporrans he wouldn't tell anyone.

119

The Scottish weather was typically uncertain this time of year. An hour earlier when he left the White Stag, it was cloudy with drizzle. Now it was dry, but a freezing wind clung to Archie's exposed face and hands, and turned his skin bright pink. His breath formed a steam vapor as he exhaled, reminding him of Gordon's hot breath.

Archie made his way down to the loch. The cruel, freezing wind had kept the usual crowd of walkers and sightseers away. Once he found the area where he had fallen in, he climbed onto the large, granite rock and looked over the edge into the dark waters.

"Gordon!" Archie shouted. "Gordon!"

He strained his eyes looking down into the water but couldn't see anything other than his own reflection. He leaned down and prodded the water's surface with his finger. Archie was surprised that it was cold but not as icy as he had remembered it the day he fell in.

"Gordon!" After no response, Archie came up with another plan. He went back to his father's boathouse and searched for a fishing rod. Maybe he could drop a fishing line down and tie something to the end to get Gordon's attention.

He didn't find a fishing rod but did find a black rubber waterproof flashlight. He turned it on and came up with a new idea. The idea seemed foolish, even to Archie, but he was sure he would be okay. Taking the flashlight with him, he set off back towards the area where he'd first seen Gordon.

After checking no one was around, Archie undressed down to his boxers. He folded his clothes up and placed them and his shoes in a neat pile in a small crevice in the rock. The last thing he wanted was someone taking them. With one final check to make sure he was not being watched, he sat down on the edge and lowered his feet in. The cold water smothered his feet. It was a bizarre feeling—cold but no colder than the air around him. If anything, the water felt warmer than the freezing air.

Holding tight to the flashlight, Archie lowered himself into the loch. He wasn't sure why he never felt nervous, and the water felt good. He pushed away from the side and treading water while he turned on the flashlight, sending out a beam of light. Archie paused before doing anything.

He told himself that this was crazy, but he swam two lengths of the swimming pool easily. *I'll just go down a little bit.* Taking a deep breath, he lowered his head, bent down, and swam down into the dark water. Within a few seconds, he was swimming straight down, his right arm outstretched in front of him holding the flashlight.

He followed the granite rock face down, looking for the entrance. The rock seemed to go down farther and farther, so he followed the beam of light from his flashlight. After what seemed like a minute, Archie noticed the rock face starting to angle out, so he looked for an opening but found nothing. Disappointed, he slowly started the ascent back to the surface.

Archie was surprised how long he could hold his breath and not feel exhausted. That's when he saw it. He had missed it coming down because an overhanging rock overlapped the entrance. You could only find it if you were coming from below. He swam into the large hole that led to a tunnel. The tunnel went on for what Archie had guessed was almost the length of a football field . . . and went on further. Archie doubted himself. Maybe this was the wrong tunnel, one that went to nowhere. He began to run out of air. He needed to take a breath.

*Do I turn around and go back or keep going?* Archie thought. His lungs screamed at him. He swam faster. *Just a bit further, and I will turn around.* He continued and was relieved his effort was rewarded. Ahead, he saw a light. He kicked harder and continued. The tunnel became shallower, and he could see the surface. As his head broke through the surface, he gasped for air.

"Archie? Is that you?" a small voice called.

Archie stood and waded out of the water into the cavern. Miner was washing himself off.

"It is you, Archie? Welcome back!" Miner said. "Hey! Archie's back!"

Archie turned off his flashlight. He was back in the huge underground cavern. The sporrans gathered around, and in the distance, Archie noticed the huge head of Gordon approaching.

"So, the legend is true," Gordon said.

"Looks like it. Hello, Archie," Jock said, running towards him. "I had hoped it was true."

Archie looked at Gordon who was frowning at him. His massive neck swung his massive head towards Archie.

"Hi, Gordon," Archie stuttered. He looked much larger and fiercer than Archie remembered. "You don't seem too pleased to see me. But it's an emergency."

"Emergency, you say?" Gordon growled. His hot breath warmed Archie.

"Thanks," Archie smiled.

"Let me tell you something, Archie. I didn't do that to warm you. I breathe fire when I'm angry."

Jock hugged Archie's leg. "I knew it was true, Archie."

"What was true?" Archie gently stroked Jock's head.

"The great legend says that if a human takes the blood or saliva of a sea dragon, he gains part of the dragon's strength. We noticed when Gordon rescued you, he cut your ankle with his teeth. His saliva must have transmitted into your open cut and spread throughout your body. How else could you swim down here without freezing to death or running out of air?"

"So am I gonna turn into a sea dragon?"

"Puh-lease! You wish!" Gordon tutted indignantly. "Not in an octillion years."

"No, Archie. Just better strength, and of course, you can hold your breath for a long time. It will get stronger as you grow older," Jock said.

Archie nodded as he took in the information but noticed Jock's eyes didn't quite meet his. Llewellyn walked towards him, beaming with a welcoming smile.

"Maybe that's why I don't need glasses now, and maybe I could be, like, an Olympic swimmer when I'm older!"

"It's not a gift to flaunt or swagger, Archie. This goes back to the beginning of time itself. You don't want anyone to know. I have studied humans. They would want to run tests on you. You must keep this to yourself. When it last happened, well it was a couple of hundred years ago. The man went onto great things, but eventually," Llewellyn paused. "I have said too much."

Archie looked disappointed. "What is the point of being stronger and good at swimming if I can't use it?"

"But you did use it, Archie. You used it to swim here. And, according to legend, as you get older, you will develop more strength," Gordon said.

"How strong will I get? Will I get bigger?"

Gordon looked up at the cavern ceiling. Archie noticed something was wrong.

"What?" Archie asked.

Gordon lowered his head back down to Archie and gazed into the boy's eyes. "I don't know. It's just a legend. Different versions tell different events. We have said far more than we should have. Now tell me what this emergency is."

Archie sat crossed-legged, and the sporrans sat down with him. Jock sat on Archie's lap, while Archie explained the events of the gargoyles gone missing, the missing baby story, and that there had been reports of cats and dogs disappearing across the country.

Gordon watched and listened with interest. Every now and then, he shook his head. Archie picked up on his movements. Gordon was clearly concerned by some of the stories he heard. When Archie finished, Jock looked up at him and smiled. "That's settled then, Archie. You can't go back up to the surface. It's too dangerous for you."

"And eat what? Just raw potatoes and carrots? I go to school and have a dad now and a best friend named Chloe."

"Chloe?" Jock said. "Chloe? Is that a girl?"

"Yes, but we're just friends."

Gordon nodded and cleared his throat by spewing a large flame up at the ceiling. "Let me tell you all something. This is worse than I first thought. If the gargoyles are coming back to life, this can only be the work of one thing."

The sporrans all gasped in harmony. Llewellyn paced up and down. He was one of the oldest sporrans in the cavern, and the wisest. The sight of the furry little creature pacing up and down amused Archie. "We knew this day would come. Gordon, can we stop it?" Llewellyn asked.

"No, we would need a miracle. The winter solstice is just two weeks away," Gordon said. "December twenty-first is when most humans will be preparing to celebrate Christmas."

"What's the winter solstice?" Archie asked.

Llewellyn turned to Archie and continued. "The winter solstice happens every year. It's an astronomical phenomenon as the earth moves around the sun. It is at that very point when the Northern Hemisphere is at the opposite point to the Southern Hemisphere."

"I have no idea what you are talking about, I'm ten-and-a-half, not eight hundred."

"Okay, I'll put it another way, Archie. Every year, at the same time, the sun is at a certain point to us. At twelve minutes and twelve seconds after nine in the morning each year, the sun rises and the moon is still visible in the early morning sky. One end of the loch gets the sunlight and over twenty miles away, the other end gets the moonlight. The center of the loch has a gravity pull. If the gargoyles congregate around the loch at exactly that time and it's a clear day, then it will come back. It will rise from the depths of the loch."

"Oh," Archie said, although he was still confused. He paused for a while before asking again. "What will come back?"

"The nuckelavee," Gordon growled.

Archie looked wide-eyed at Gordon. "But you can defeat him, right?"

Gordon looked away. "No."

Jock explained: "Only one creature on the planet can stare at the nuckelavee and make it run and hide. And that creature is the smartest, prettiest, and most brilliant creature on the entire planet."

Gordon's massive head swooped down within an inch of Jock; his hot breath was uncomfortable for Archie. "You have a big mouth for such a small sporran."

Jock gulped. "I w—w—w—was j—just stating a fact. The nuckelavee is afraid of sporrans."

Archie sat quietly trying to piece everything together. "So, let me get this straight. The gargoyles can eat sporrans. Gordon can turn the gargoyles to stone. But only sporrans can defeat the nuckelavee?"

"Exactly," Gordon said. "If the nuckelavee returns, he will first call on a swarm of gargoyles that can sniff out a sporran from a hundred miles away."

"Is there any way to kill the nuckelavee?" Archie asked.

Llewellyn walked forward. "No," he paused. "Okay, there is, but practically impossible for it to happen."

"What is it?" Archie asked.

"The legend says that the nuckelavee can only be killed if it is burnt by the fire of a petrified tree. And let's face it, the odds of finding such a tree are low, and if you do, then you have to ask the nuckelavee to climb it or stand next to it and then burn it."

Archie climbed to his feet, taking Jock with him. "Sorry, Gordon, but your breath is burning me." He sat down again a few feet further back. "We need to come up with a plan."

"I did," Jock said. "We all stay down here. That includes you, Archie. It's safe."

"What about all the children in the village or all the other villages across Great Britain? We can't let them become gargoyle grub. I have friends at my new school who I like," Archie paused. "And there are some I don't like, but even they don't deserve to be some ugly gargoyle's supper."

## Chapter Fourteen

Another two hours conferring brought them no closer to a plan. Archie agreed to come back down again in a few days. In the meantime, he would monitor news reports and sightings of gargoyles.

His swim back to the surface was uneventful. He was happy to see his clothing was where he had hid it. He made a mental note that next time he would wear his swim shorts so he didn't have to go home wearing wet underwear under his clothes. He sneaked home hoping no one would see had a wet patch coming through his trousers, giving the impression he had peed himself.

After changing, he flicked on the TV and waited for the news to come on. The main story was regarding an oil spill from a tanker in the Atlantic Ocean. Another story was the one Archie had been dreading. A poultry farmer in Northern England had his entire flock destroyed by what they suspected was a large pack of foxes or dogs. The farmer's own dog was missing, and as for the chickens, thousands of feathers were the only evidence.

Another story was given less importance but meant more to Archie. In Glasgow, an infant was snatched from its crib. Police suspected it was the work of a woman who wanted a baby. Archie suspected something far worse. Worse still, the incidents were getting closer to Scotland.

*

Foyers Junior School was putting on its annual Christmas play. This year was Charles Dickens's *The Christmas Carol*, although they called it *Scrooge*. Archie was given the part of Fred, Ebenezer Scrooge's nephew. Chloe had a part in the play as Scrooge's ex-girlfriend, Belle. Both Archie and Chloe had a few words to say, and both were nervous on the evening of the play.

Most of the village turned out to watch the performance. Archie was surprised how much he enjoyed being part of the village. As the son of Alec McIntosh, he had been immediately accepted, although a few boys in his class had purposely bumped into him. Now and again, they would mimic his English accent, but for the most part, though, he had been welcomed.

A few performers forgot their lines and had to be prompted. Thomas, who was playing Bob Marley's ghost, tripped over his chains and fell off the stage, much to the amusement of some. But, overall, the play was a success. After, Archie was leaving with his dad when there was a small commotion at the school gate. Chloe looked upset and her mother comforted her.

"Chloe, what's wrong?" Archie asked, rushing to her. He thought she was about to burst into tears at any second.

"It's Angus. We tied his lead up to the gate during the play, and he's gone!" Chloe sniffed, holding back her tears.

"Did he break the lead?" Archie's father asked.

"No, the collar is broken," Evan said, studying the collar. "I'm sure he will be at home, Chloe. Don't worry. He's a good dog and will find his way home."

"Do you think so?" Chloe asked.

Archie was looking elsewhere, searching the rooftops.

"Come on. Evan's right. Let's go home. I bet he'll be home wagging his tail and looking pleased with himself," Chloe's mom said. "And I'll buy everyone a portion of chips on the way. That'll keep us warm."

Chloe, Evan, and Archie waited outside the fish-and-chip shop while their parents bought chips.

"What are you getting for Christmas, Archie?" Evan asked.

Archie looked at him, unsure what to make of Evan. He could be horrid one moment and really nice the next. Archie never had any brothers or sisters, and he wondered if they were all like that to each other. Both Evan and Chloe seemed to spend time annoying the life out of each other, yet if anyone would dare to hurt Chloe, Evan would die to protect her. And when someone said something bad about Evan, Chloe gave them a tongue-lashing.

"I was hoping to get a kite like you have. A dual-line kite."

"Then you had better be good and not go falling in the loch again and scaring me half to death," Alec said, passing him a bag of chips.

Archie unwrapped them and blew on a chip before popping it in his mouth. "What are you getting, Evan?"

"An iPad. Aren't, I mom?"

"You will have to see," Evan's mother snapped. "Come. Don't dillydally. We want to make sure Angus went home."

"With computers and iPads, we'll no longer need paper." Evan said. "It'll save a lot of trees."

"Ha! Well, I don't think they will take the place of *all* paper, laddie. I'd like to see you take an iPad into the bathroom and wipe your backside with it," Archie's dad said, laughing. Everyone joined him in the hilarity.

As they approached the end of North Street, Archie and his dad took the left turn to their cottage, while Evan, Chloe, and their mother took the other street home. Of course, Archie's fears were accurate: Angus was not seen again. Archie suspected Angus had been taken by gargoyles. If he was correct, they could be watching him and his father right then.

Archie spent a few days coming up with a plan. In his bedroom, he put pictures of the loch on his walls. He kept articles from newspapers that mentioned missing animals, children, and, of course, church-roof gargoyles that were disappearing.

As the weekend approached, he agreed to go out with Chloe and search for Angus. He thought it would be fruitless, but she was his best friend and he couldn't say no. They walked for just over a mile, keeping to the footpath of the loch. As they both shouted for Angus, Archie sensed that, deep down, Chloe knew she would never see her dog again. But searching for him gave her comfort, knowing she was doing something.

"How far have we walked?" Chloe asked, kicking a pebble across the path.

"I dunno . . . probably two miles. It looks like it's gonna rain, so maybe we should head back?"

Chloe nodded, and they turned and started the walk back to Foyers. The December weather in Scotland was uncertain; heavy rain clouds formed overhead. Typically, without warning, the downpour brought with it an angry wind, which did its best to aggravate the waters of the loch.

The storm front towered above them. Archie and Chloe were caught in its grasp. Lightning lit up the sky, followed by an intense crack of thunder.

"Go ahead, you big wuss! Lightning bolt my back side if you're so big," Chloe shouted up at the sky, bent over and wriggling her backside.

"Are you crazy? You might actually get struck," Archie said laughing, pulling her off the path and under an alder tree for shelter.

"You're not afraid of the lightning, are you?" Chloe shouted above the storm.

"No, but we don't want to get soaked through or end up extra crispy fried if we do get struck by lightning!" Archie noticed Chloe's face change. Her eyes as wide as saucers and her mouth dropped open to an adorable little O. She was looking behind him and looked petrified. Archie swung around to see what she was looking at.

## Chapter Fifteen

He came face-to-face with the most hideous, grotesque creature he had ever seen. Slowly walking towards them, on bony, twisted legs, was a gargoyle. Five feet tall, it stood taller than Archie. It had the wings of a bat, and the head looked part-lion, part-gorilla with exaggerated teeth. Archie was paralyzed to the spot. The gargoyle was brutal and terrifying, like nothing he had seen or would want to see in his worst nightmare. Shaking uncontrollably, on instinct, Archie forced himself to breathe.

The gargoyle was focused on Chloe, thick salvia dripping from its mouth. Its body was covered with a translucent, glossy skin, so thin that the gargoyle's muscles and bones were clearly defined from the entire length of its body to its wings. Its feet had massive dirty claws protruding from its toes.

Chloe and Archie watched in disbelief as it came closer, just an arm's length away. It tilted its head and almost grinned in excitement at the thought of its coming meal. Archie didn't know why he did, but he felt the need to protect Chloe. His legs felt like they were stuck to the ground. He forced himself to step in front of her and look at the gargoyle. Archie gulped, his legs trembling with fear. A tense silence fell over them. The air itself quivered with anticipation.

The gargoyle moved its head and eyes as if in slow motion to focus on Archie. The creature's tongue slipped through its lower teeth and curled up, trying to taste Archie's scent. It looked Archie in the eye.

Hastily, it took a step back and, from deep in its stomach, gave an ear-deafening scream that sounded like a cross between the caw of a crow and the trumpet of an African elephant.

Chloe caught hold of Archie's arm for protection and to stop herself from collapsing. The gargoyle recoiled further, turning its body away, trying to shield itself with its wings. Archie took Chloe's hand, and for a split second, he took his eyes off the gargoyle. It lunged forward but stopped short when Archie looked at it. Again, it backed off, hissing in disgust at the boy.

*He's afraid of me!* Archie said to himself. Flushed with the feeling of power, Archie released Chloe's hand and took a step forward.

"Grrah! Grah! Go away," Archie growled, waving his arms up in the air.

The gargoyle recoiled, flapped its enormous wings, displaying a sharp claw on the tips, and flew into the stormy sky, making more squawking sounds.

For a few moments, Archie and Chloe stood in silence looking up into the sky. It was gone.

"C'mon. Let's get home," Archie said, still looking up.

"Archie, you were so brave. I'm just happy I didn't pee myself."

"I'm so wet now with the rain, I wouldn't know if I had anyway," Archie said, pulling Chloe with him. They ran back to Foyers.

"What was it? Do you think that was the Loch Ness Monster?" Chloe asked.

"Nah, that was just a gargoyle."

Chloe pulled Archie back and stopped.

"*Just* a gargoyle? Oh my gosh! They've been on the news. I didn't think they were real. Was it real or am I dreaming? Did you really just tell that ugly bat with a lion's head to go away?"

"Well, I wasn't going to invite him for dinner. I think we were on the menu."

"Wait until I tell Evan what you did. He won't call you names again."

They continued running, and a few paces later, Archie asked, "What does Evan call me?"

"Don't take any notice of him. He's my big brother and he is bound to be protective of me."

"What does he call me?"

"Well, you did say you could only swim ten meters. It turns out you can swim over a hundred *and* underwater."

"What did he call me?" Archie insisted.

"Not a name really. He said I shouldn't trust anyone who lies."

"Oh." Archie said. "I never lied. I could only swim ten meters until . . ." He trailed off. "I can't say. It's a secret."

They had made it back to Foyers, between a few scattered homes on the outskirts, feeling safe enough to walk and take a shortcut through the cemetery. Unlike most people who would feel uneasy or even scared of walking through a graveyard, Archie loved the feeling of knowing that not everyone can walk out.

"You have to promise you won't tell anyone what just happened," Archie said.

Chloe knocked him on the side of his head. She wiped the rainwater from his face. "Are you crazy? Of course we have to tell everyone. The whole village, police, the army, the Prime minister, and maybe even the Queen."

"And say what exactly? A gargoyle flew down from the sky, I said boo, and it flew away again. Yeah, I can see that working. They'll think you're nuts. Probably put you in a home and lock you up and throw away the key."

"Not if we both tell them what we saw."

"What did you see exactly?" a deep Scottish voice said from directly behind them. Both Archie and Chloe jumped.

Mr. MacGregor stood over them. Archie never noticed it before when he had pulled him out the loch, but Mr. MacGregor looked old, older than anyone he had ever seen before. Even his clothing looked old, but older than what you would expect to see an old man wearing. He wore a kilt, with matching tartan slung over his shoulder and two leather belts, one around his waist and one over his shoulder. His socks came to his knees, grey in color with green garters like the Boy Scouts wear. The rain fell off him without penetrating his clothing. Archie and Chloe froze to the spot.

"I asked a question. What did you kids see? Was it the *beast*?" Mr. MacGregor asked, his eyes widening.

"What beast?" Archie asked.

"The beast of the loch. The Loch Ness Monster!"

"It's just a myth," Chloe snapped back.

Mr. MacGregor eyed both children suspiciously. "Aye. Some say it's a myth. Others have seen it and seen what it can do and how it can wreck a man's life." His voice was sad. He looked away and gazed at the loch.

Chloe pulled Archie's arm and led him away. When they were out of earshot, she whispered to him. "He's crazy. You know that, don't you? My granddad said Mr. MacGregor was drunk one night in the White Stag and told people how the Loch Ness Monster ate his cattle. He said it cost him everything . . . his wife and his reputation."

"Exactly. That's why we can't say we saw the gargoyle," Archie said. "We don't want people saying we're crazy."

# Chapter Sixteen

Chloe didn't attend school on Monday. Her mother informed the school her daughter had come down with a cold after getting caught in a downpour looking for her lost dog. Archie never would have admitted it, but he missed having her at school. He realized that she was really the only friend he had at Foyers. The school day seemed to go much slower. That was, until the afternoon history lesson. They were covering Scottish history, and Mrs. Duncan was very enthusiastic teaching the lesson. She told the story of one of Scotland's most famous heroes: Rob Roy.

"Who here has seen the movie *Rob Roy*, starring Liam Neeson?" she cheerfully asked the class.

All hands went up apart from Archie's. He had never seen the movie and had no idea who Liam Neeson was.

Mrs. Duncan went on to explain that, at the age of eighteen, Rob Roy joined his father and other clansmen in battles to protect the land against the Spanish. Later in life, he became a cattleman, until he failed to repay a loan. Legend said the head rancher stole his cattle, others said the English took them. Some even said he had became hooked on whisky, became a drunk, and told people the Loch Ness Monster ate them. At this point the children laughed. They had heard many strange tales about Nessie, mostly stories told for the amusement of tourists.

Archie was more interested than most in the history lesson. After school, he went to see Chloe, who was pleased to see him but embarrassed she was wearing her Minnie Mouse pajamas and fluffy, penguin-faced slippers.

"I missed you at school and wanted to make sure you were okay," Archie said.

"I got a cold," Chloe said in a muffled voice through a blocked stuffy nose.

"Will you want to stay for dinner, Archie?" Chloe's mom asked.

"Um. If that's okay. Yes, please. I'm sure it will be better than what Chef Mike cooks."

"*Chef Mike*. Your father has a chef named Mike who prepares your dinner?"

Archie blushed and bit his bottom lip. "Not exactly. Chef Mike is what dad calls the microwave. He normally serves up a microwave dinner. I better call him and let him know, or else he will think I have fallen in the Loch again."

Archie followed Chloe up to her room. He hid his grin as he entered; she had posters of the band One Direction and other posters of cute puppies and kittens. Her room was mostly pink and yellow. It was the first time he had been in a girl's room. She hurried in and picked up clothing on the floor and hid a pile under the bed.

"Do you know who Rob Roy is?" Archie asked.

"You mean *was*. Yeah, he's a Scottish hero." Chloe sat on her bed.

"We covered him in history today—"

"Boring. I don't want to talk about school. Has anyone else seen the gargoyle?"

"Do you know Rob Roy's full name?"

Chloe sighed. "No, but I'm sure you're going to tell me anyway."

"It's Rob Roy *MacGregor*. In history, they said that he had become a cattleman and a herdsman stole his herd. Legend says he told people the Loch Ness Monster ate his cattle."

She looked at him, her eyes widening. "Do you think Mr. MacGregor is related to him, like his great-great grandson?"

"You told me your grandmother was afraid of him when she was little. He was old back then, so how come he is still alive? He must be way over a hundred if he was an old man when your grandmother was a little girl. I think Mr. MacGregor is Rob Roy."

Chloe burst out laughing. "Now, who's going to be called crazy and put in a home?"

"He told us Gordon—I mean Nessie ate his cattle. How else is he still alive?"

"Gordon?" Chloe asked.

Archie sighed looking down at the floor and fiddled with his fingers. "If I tell you something, you must promise not to tell anyone."

"Of course, we're best friends."

"I mean it, you can't tell anyone. This is a huge secret and hard to believe. I can hardly believe it myself."

Chloe raised her small finger. "Pinky promise."

Archie raised his little finger to hers as both fingers grasped each other. They shook their hands up and down and, in harmony, gave the pinky swear.

"Pinky promise,

"Pinky swear,

"If I tell,

"I'll get eaten by a bear."

Archie explained everything to Chloe: how he fell into the loch, about the sporrans, Gordon, the cut on his ankle, his new ability to swim further, and that he no longer needed glasses. The nuckelavee and the gargoyles. When he finished she sat looking at him, and her blue eyes sparkled like sapphires.

"If I hadn't seen the gargoyle myself I would have said you are a raving lunatic and should be locked up. I can believe all of it except the bit about Mr. MacGregor. He would have to be over two hundred and eighty years old. No one can live that long," she paused. "Unless?"

"Unless what?" Archie asked.

"Well, you mentioned that the sporrans told you Nessie—sorry, I mean Gordon—had scratched someone before. What if Rob Roy MacGregor had tried to protect his cattle and somehow got bitten by Gordon. Maybe he is the other human, and he has powers like you, and one of those powers is to live forever."

"It's possible, but one thing I forgot to mention: In history today, Mrs. Duncan told us that he was buried in a place called Kirkyard." Archie scratched his head.

"I've been there. Just a tourist place. They also say his sons are buried there, but my dad says it's not true, because his sons died years later. It is set up for tourists to visit and take pictures, just like they do here trying to catch a glimpse of the Loch Ness Monster."

They both sat quietly for a minute, and it was Archie who spoke first. "I have to speak to Gordon again. Maybe tomorrow after school." He looked at Chloe. "But don't tell anyone. I'll let my dad know I'm coming to see you."

"This isn't gonna end well, sneaking around and telling lies."

Her mother called them both down for dinner. Chloe didn't have an appetite and picked at her food. What she didn't eat Evan willingly took.

## Chapter Seventeen

The following day, after school, Archie dropped by his father's workshop and informed him he was going to see Chloe and that he'd do his homework later. He had other plans, of course, and crossed his fingers behind his back while he lied. Somehow, that seemed to make it right in Archie's mind. He went home, grabbed his swim shorts, flashlight, and a towel, and went back to the boulder by the loch.

After checking the coast was clear, he hurriedly changed his clothing and jumped in. The long swim down was uneventful at the start, but as soon as he found the entrance, he had the shock of his life: Gordon was on his way out. Gordon had to stop himself from snapping at Archie as he mistook him for a large fish.

Archie froze, seeing Gordon's huge mouth snap at him. Eventually, the lack of oxygen brought him back to his senses. Archie continued into the cavern and climbed out, followed by Gordon.

"Are you *crazy*? You nearly ate me," Archie shouted angrily.

Gordon coughed a large flame. It lit up the entrance to the cavern. A scurry of sporrans had heard Archie shouting and came to see him.

"Let me tell you something," Gordon began in his usual manner. "You looked like a pike. Your skin is so white and you're so small and thin I thought I had an easy snack. And what's that on your clothing," Gordon's head came close to Archie's shorts.

Archie looked down at his bright blue shorts with orange clown fish designs on them. "Oh. That's Nemo. He's a cartoon character from the movie *Finding Nemo*. It's about this clown fish called Nemo and . . ." Archie trailed off. "Well, it's not a real fish. You should be able to tell the difference."

"Let me tell you something, Archie. You looked like a large pike with a small fish swimming along your waist. Sorry if I scared you, but I don't eat humans."

"Well, I was going to ask you about that. Did you ever bite a man called Rob Roy MacGregor?" The sporrans gasped and looked worried. "I take that as a yes?"

"No." Gordon sighed. "Okay, yes. Let me tell you, it was an unusually hot summer and fishing was hard. I noticed a few cattle liked to come down to drink at the loch. It was easy food for me. I could take one or two a day. Cows are very tasty. I can see why humans eat them.

"One particular day this crazy cattleman came at me, out of nowhere, wielding a huge sword. He tried to stab me with it. I was too quick for him. I snapped the sword and picked him up by his legs and threw him out into the loch. He swam back but I must have bitten his leg in the process."

Llewellyn continued the story. "That man is the human we spoke of. He went off and told people that the Loch Ness M-word had eaten his cattle and attacked him. Of course, no one believed him."

"Do you know what happened to him?"

"He's fine, Archie. He helped you out of the water the other day. He was not injured too bad," Gordon said.

"*Fine*. He's not *fine*. He's like three hundred years old!"

The sporrans and Gordon all looked at each other. It was Jock who spoke first. "What's wrong with that?"

"Humans aren't supposed to live that long. Does that mean I will live to be that old? Thinking about it means I will spend most of my life as a grey, winkled old man."

Llewellyn noticed Archie looked troubled. He stepped forward. "Don't regret growing older, but remember, it's a privilege that is denied to many."

Sporrans don't really have shoulders, but Jock shrugged his body.

"All my family, friends, and future children and grandchildren will die before me," Archie said. "Mr. MacGregor is very lonely. He must have seen all his family die over the years."

"Isn't that better than being in a concrete garden?" Miner asked.

"What's that?"

"The concrete garden. You humans dig holes, put the dead in boxes and bury them, and then you place a concrete pillar on top. Living must be better than being stuck in a box with a concrete pillar on top."

"Oh, you mean a cemetery or graveyard. I'm not sure what is worse. Anyway, that's not why I really came back down here. I saw a gargoyle. I was with Chloe. I think it was going to eat us, but it was scared of me.".

"Let me tell you something. Of course it was scared of you. You have my DNA running through your veins now," Gordon said.

"Then why are you scared of the M-word?" Archie asked.

"I'm afraid of nothing."

"Really, well some people think gargoyles look like *monsters*," Archie said, making sure he said monster in a louder voice.

"Monsters!" shrieked Gordon, looking around from side to side. He reared up and tried to hide his face with his front claws.

"Gordon, he was joking. Calm down," Jock smiled.

"Oh. He has jokes?" Gordon growled, his head moving close to Archie, as he sniffed the boy. "You actually still look quite appetizing in your—What was it? Nemo shorts."

Archie apologized and explained everything regarding the gargoyle. They were uncertain what to do. Archie felt for sure that Llewellyn would have an idea.

Suddenly a green puff of smoke appeared from behind Gordon. He looked guilty. "Fire in the hole," he hollowed.

"Oh my. Gordon you just did a booty belch," Jock said, waving both hands in front of him trying to push away the air that Gordon had just polluted.

"*Gordon*. That stinks," Archie said holding his nose. "So that's what sea dragon fart smells like. Yuk."

"Sorry. I came across a delicious shoal of stickleback fish. They always have that effect on me."

"Well, just don't breathe any fire for a minute, or you'll blow us all up," Archie said, grinning.

As for the gargoyle problem, none of the sporrans knew what to do, so it fell on Archie to come up with a plan. "Gordon, you are just going to have to come up and stare at them and screech or whatever you do. You have to turn them back to stone."

"I can't do that. The nuckelavee is too close, and what if I get seen by a human? They will be back with more boats and small submarines looking for me, fishing and eating all my food."

Nothing Archie could do or say would make Gordon take any action. Since it was so close to the winter solstice, Gordon was afraid. Eventually Archie gave up. He spent time chatting to Jock and, in due course, swam back up to the surface. Archie was disappointed in Gordon and the sporrans. They were all older than him, much older, but they had all left it up to him to try and think of something.

\*

When Archie got home, his father had made hot stew for dinner. Well, that's what he told Archie, but Archie saw the empty stew cans in the trash.

"Before you eat dinner, go up to your room, Archie. I went into Inverness today and I have a surprise for you," Alec said.

Archie ran up the stairs two at a time. He was expecting his new kite. On his bed, he noticed new clothing: a white shirt, long socks, a black jacket and something that horrified him.

His father followed him up into his room. "What do ya think, Archie? It's our family's McIntosh tartan."

"It's a kilt," Archie said in disgust.

"Of course it is. On the Sunday before Christmas, the whole village goes to the church service. All the men wear kilts. I shall be wearing mine. All of your friends at school will be as well."

"But I'm not Scottish," Archie said, prodding the kilt with his finger as if it was something dead.

"Of course you are. Okay, maybe fifty-percent Scottish, but as you live here now, you are more Scottish than English. Try it on."

Archie picked up the kilt and held it out in front of him. "I'll look like a girl."

With his father's help, he tried on his new clothing and looked at himself in the mirror. Archie wouldn't admit it, but he liked what he saw. He was looking forward to fitting in with everyone else. Chloe had already told him her father and Evan would be wearing a kilt.

"I didn't get a sporran for you, because not all the young boys wear them. Maybe I'll get one for you another year. Now back into your old clothes, and let's have some of my homemade stew."

Archie checked his father when he mentioned the stew. He never had his fingers crossed and he was lying. He suspected adults didn't have to cross their fingers when they told white lies.

## Chapter Eighteen

The front page of every newspaper was the same news story as the TV news. Up and down the country, gargoyles had gone missing from rooftops. Some suspected copycat thieves or a large gang of antique hunters. Only the older gargoyles were missing.

Archie watched the news. He was sure the reason the new gargoyles weren't missing was because they were actually made of concrete. It was only the very old ones that had been turned to stone by Gordon's shriek hundreds of years ago.

At school, Chloe got into a fight with ten-year-old Jimmy Johnson. He had been teasing her, mostly commenting that Archie was her boyfriend. He called her "Southern Softie Lover." In defending Archie, she lost her quick temper and punched Jimmy Johnson on the nose, giving him a nosebleed.

Both Chloe and Jimmy Johnson sat outside Mrs. Taggert's office. Copper-haired Jimmy, one of the tallest boys in the school, was holding a blood-stained handkerchief to his nose. His small dark eyes seemed to be too close together and he had two missing front teeth and a squat nose. Jimmy Johnson had most defiantly been hit with the ugly stick several times. He was loud and often threw his weight around to make himself the main attraction. He often picked on someone and made fun of them. Today it was Chloe's turn. Chloe was having none of it and slammed her fist into Jimmy's wet nose.

Mrs. Taggert appeared from her office, looked at Chloe and Jimmy over the top of her glasses, and tutted. "Chloe, in my office," she ordered, pointing at her door as if it was a mile away. To make her point, Mrs. Taggert slammed her door and walked around behind her desk. She gave Chloe another stare over the top of her glasses. If looks could kill, rigor mortis would have set into Chloe's body by then.

"What is our policy on fighting in school?" Mrs. Taggert asked.

"But Jimmy Johnson was teasing me!"

"What is our policy on fighting?" Mrs. Taggert shouted so loudly they probably heard her in China.

Chloe jumped. She was upset to be in the office, but was not about to cry or give in. "We should not fight," she said softly.

"Exactly. Under no circumstances do we fight. What kind of young lady will you become if you go around hitting boys?"

Chloe opened her mouth to argue, she decided to keep her thoughts to herself. "Sorry, Mrs. Taggert."

After another five minutes of being told how to act and in the future to report any bullying, Chloe was then sent back to class.

Jimmy denied any wrongdoing, as he always did. Mrs. Taggert had known him since he started at the school when he was five, and according to him, it was always someone else's fault.

Both Jimmy and Chloe had to write two pages on why it was bad to fight or name call at school. The work had to be done over the weekend.

As school broke up for the day, Jimmy noticed Archie in the corridor. He marched up and looked down at him. "Southern Softie, it's your fault I got extra homework. Why don't you go back to England and leave Scotland for the Scots?"

"I'm half-Scottish. My dad is Scottish," Archie said. He suspected Jimmy actually liked Chloe and was jealous of him.

"Are you arguing with me? You wanna make something of it? I'll see you, Archie." Jimmy stuck out his chest and took a step forward.

"No, leave me alone. I've not done anything to you," Archie said, squeezing his way past Jimmy and to the school gate.

Archie's evolutionary mechanism that all humans have to keep us alert when we are being watched had been triggered. He had the feeling tugging at him, and he wanted to turn around and confront his follower but hoped Jimmy would stop following him. Archie was never one to pick a fight but there are times when even the mildest of people could be drawn into one. He thought it pointless to fight with Jimmy. After all, Jimmy was an ugly brute and had nothing to lose. He was already missing two front teeth and had a broken nose. Jimmy once boasted he got his broken nose from fighting off a gang of boys. But Chloe told him Jimmy had simply been showing off one day on his bicycle riding with no hands and rode head first into a tree.

As he left the exit of the school grounds, Archie, sensing he was being followed, tried speeding up. As he rounded the corner, Jimmy shouted at him.

"No point running, Southern Softie, I'll catch ya."

Archie stopped and turned around. "Leave me alone. I have to get home."

"I think you're asking to get your head kicked in!"

"I speak English and can understand most Scottish accents, but I don't speak Loser Language," Archie said, but as soon as he did, he wished he had kept his mouth shut.

Before Archie could say anything else, Jimmy launched himself, catching Archie around the neck and holding him in a headlock under his left arm. His right fist punched Archie's face twice. Archie tugged his head trying to get free, but unable to do so, Archie grabbed Jimmy's fist to stop the pummeling. He squeezed Jimmy's fist and kept squeezing.

"Agh! Stop it. Let go!" Jimmy yelled, relaxing his grip on Archie's neck.

But, Archie's grip got tighter. He was now free from Jimmy's clutches and continued to squeeze Jimmy's fist so hard Jimmy's fingers turned white.

Jimmy fell to his knees in agonizing pain. "Please stop! I'm sorry, Archie. I won't call you 'Southern Softie' again. Stop!"

A small group of children watched as the school bully became a quivering wreck while the smaller Archie crushed his hand.

"Aye, that'll be enough to teach him. Now let him go, laddie," a deep Scottish voice said from behind Archie. Archie turned. It was Mr. MacGregor.

Tears streamed down Jimmy's face, and he begged Archie to release his grip. Archie continued to squeeze. Mr. MacGregor leaned in close to Archie and stared at him. Unaware of his new strength, Archie was almost afraid to let Jimmy go in case Jimmy hit him again.

"Let him go, boy," Mr. MacGregor said.

Archie looked in disbelief at Mr. MacGregor's eyes. They slowly changed from a pale grey to bright orange. Mr. MacGregor pried Archie's hand off Jimmy's fist. Jimmy rubbed his fist and climbed to his feet and backed away. Mr. MacGregor squeezed Archie's fingers hard.

"Let me go," Archie said, pulling away.

"See! You don't like it yourself, do you?" Mr. MacGregor smiled, taking delight in hurting Archie. That was until he noticed Archie's eyes, which suddenly—and just for a split second—also turned orange.

Mr. MacGregor let the boy go as if he had been given an electric shock. He took a step back, his was shaking, looking wide-eyed.

Archie shrugged off the incident and continued his journey home, though he wondered why Mr. MacGregor's eyes turned orange, the same bright color as Gordon's. He had to let Chloe know. He was also surprised he had managed to beat Jimmy Johnson. He put it down to his new strength. It made him wonder about all sorts of things he might be able to do.

*I wonder if I should get a cloak like Batman or Superman. I could travel around to different schools and take on all the school bullies,* Archie thought to himself. He tried to come up with a possible superhero name. At first, he thought he could be "A-B Boy" for "Anti-Bully Boy." Then other names came into his thoughts, such as "Bully Basher" or "Archie the Avenger" and even "Super Boy."

He later told himself that was ridiculous. He wasn't going to be eleven until May. He had no ability to fly and, so far, had only been able to swim fast, hold his breath for a long while, see farther and clearer, and be stronger than anyone his age.

Evan caught up with him. "Archie!"

He turned and noticed Evan carrying a large bag.

"Hey! Is Chloe okay?" Archie asked.

"Yeah she's doin' fine, but she asked me to give you this." Evan held out the bag. "I wore it to the school Christmas dance a few years ago, so I'm sure it will fit you."

Archie took the bag and peered inside. "What is it?"

"We didn't think you would have a costume for the school dance, and a few years ago, I went as a pirate." Evan smiled.

"Oh. Wow! I never knew it was a dress-up dance like that. I've only ever dressed up in a costume at Halloween."

"Foyers School's Christmas dance is always fancy dress. Last year, Chloe went as Snow White. I went as Jack Frost from *Frozen*. I had flour in my hair and everything. This year, I'm going as James Bond."

"Oh, thanks. My dad would have had no idea what to put me in. He'd probably wrap me in a white sheet and tell me to go as a ghost. Thanks, Evan. I can't wait. It's gonna be wicked."

"Oh yeah, it's gonna be wicked, all right." Evan's eyes narrowed as he smiled.

# Chapter Nineteen

The night of the school party, Archie was excited. He had never been to a fancy-dress party before. He wondered what Chloe was going to dress up as. He dressed in the tight jeans ripped off just below the knee and the white striped shirt Evan gave him. He placed the black patch over his right eye and switched it to his left before making his way downstairs. His father was reading the paper, and for the first time, Archie heard his father curse.

"That greedy Green Oil Company that Chloe's dad works for. They want to bring an oil pipe through Loch Ness. They say it will have less of an environmental impact. 'Better than digging up the roads,' they say. More like it will make more profits, and they don't care if it leaks and pollutes the loch." He threw the paper in the trash and looked at Archie. "Ah, Jim, lad," his dad said in a deep pirate voice.

"What's the best eye to wear the patch over?" Archie asked.

"It's fine where it is. Let me help you with the head scarf." Alec wrapped the red headscarf around Archie's head and tied it at the back. Archie wore a belt and tucked the wooden sword down the front of it. His left hand slipped into a sleeve with a plastic hook at the end. After his father clipped a red soft toy parrot to Archie's shoulder, Archie examined himself in the mirror.

"The parrot flops to one side," he complained.

"I can't get it to sit straight. Well, it's a pirate's parrot, and he's been drinking rum and got drunk," his father joked, and drew a moustache on Archie's face with the black face paint and went to fetch his camera.

After taking a few pictures posing in front of the Christmas tree, some waving the sword and some with the "hang loose" sign with his right hand, Archie was ready to go.

"Archie, it's six o'clock. You better get going, or you'll be late."

"I'm on my way," Archie said, pulling on his sneakers.

Archie walked with his father to school. As they approached, he could hear laughter. Evan and his friends stood at the gate with white sheets wrapped around them.

Archie looked at his dad. "I can go in on my own, Dad. Thanks for bringing me."

"Okay, son. Have a nice time. I will be back at nine to pick you up."

Archie made his way to Evan and his friends, who were still laughing.

"Why've you got sheets around you?" Archie asked.

"We keep our costumes hidden until we go in, and then reveal ourselves," James said. Evan was looking away. Archie noticed Evan was shaking. He assumed Evan must have been cold. Or was he laughing?

Archie couldn't put his finger on it, but something didn't seem quite right. He shrugged it off. He was delighted to be with the older boys and treated as equal.

He followed the four of them into the school. Evan suggested Archie get between the four of them and stay hidden until inside the school. This way, his costume would also be a secret until he was in the main school hall. The four boys stood in a square with Archie between them. They kept him well squashed so he couldn't see much. They were all taller than him, and the sheets they had on almost covered him as well.

The school hall was decorated in a Christmas theme. The lights were low, but spotlights shone around the room and pulsing lights from the DJ's equipment lit up the room. The music was very loud, but Archie liked it.

"Okay, let's reveal," James said. The four boys all dropped the sheets. Archie was stunned. They were all wearing black pants, white shirts, and ties.

"What costume is that?' Archie said, as his voice trailed off.

"We are young James Bonds," Evan said, laughing. They parted, allowing everyone to see Archie.

He was horrified. Everyone looked at him, pointing and laughing. Archie stood in the middle of the dance floor dressed as a pirate holding a toy wooden sword, while every other boy was dressed in a shirt and pants and the girls in pretty party dresses. Evan and his friends roared with laughter, followed by others in the room.

Jimmy walked up to Archie. "Ha! You look like a three-year-old. Now who's a loser?"

Archie dropped the sword and ran outside, tears streaming down his face. Chloe chased after him.

"Archie, slow down," she called out.

He ran down towards the loch, his tears turning to anger. He ripped off the parrot and his headscarf, and threw them on the ground. He kicked a rock and shouted abuse at the sky.

"Archie!" Chloe said, when she finally caught up with him.

"I suppose you think that was funny!" Archie screamed at her.

She walked closer to him and picked up the headscarf. She wiped his tears. "Whatever gave you the idea it was a costume party?"

"Evan said *you* told him to let me wear his pirate costume," Archie said. He was so angry he almost cursed.

"And you believe I'd do that? I had nothing to do with it. You have been tricked, Archie. I would never do that."

"He said it was your idea."

"And who do you believe . . . him or me?"

"Neither of you. I hate this stupid school and this stupid country. England is much better and not so cold. My real friends in London would never be so cruel." He tore off his eye patch and T-shirt, and threw them at her, before storming off, wearing just the cutoff jeans.

Chloe picked up the clothing and went back towards the school almost in tears. Archie walked through the village towards the loch. Garbage cans were still full, spilling their leftovers onto the pavement, waiting for to tomorrow's pick up. A large rat sat on the top of one, its whiskers twitching at the air as it watched Archie walked past.

# Chapter Twenty

Archie sat down on a rock overlooking the loch, which was calm, its black surface reflecting the moonlight, overcast sky. He cried and felt pretty miserable although thought he might have been wrong about Chloe. It was Evan's idea, and maybe she *was* innocent. Just as he started to feel guilty, he heard footsteps behind him.

"Catch yourself a death of cold sitting out here with no shirt and coat you will, laddie." Mr. MacGregor sat down next to Archie and passed him a handkerchief.

"Thanks." Archie sniffed.

"Och. That's what tears are for, to wash away pain and ease the hate." Mr. MacGregor touched Archie's bare shoulder. Behind the wild and wiry bush of sideburns, he wore a very kind smile. "I'm guessing you don't feel the cold much now."

Archie wiped his eyes and nodded at him. MacGregor wore the same clothes he always wore and carried his walking stick—what they called a *shillelagh*.

"So, I was right. You have been cursed by the demon of the loch?" Mr. MacGregor said, shaking his head.

"He's called Gordon," Archie said as a matter of fact.

"Who is?"

"Nessie. The Loch Ness Monster. He's actually called 'Gordon'."

"Call him what you want laddie, but he's a demon all right. Mark my words."

"*I* don't call him that. That's his name. I've spoken to him. Just like you did."

Mr. MacGregor studied the boy. "Did you hit your head, boy? You can't speak to the beast. It'll eat you alive."

"You're Rob Roy MacGregor, aren't you?" A smile came back to Archie's face.

Mr. MacGregor sighed and looked at his head of the *shillelagh* as if he was looking into a crystal ball. "It's been a few hundred years since someone called me Rob Roy."

Archie beamed as if he had won a gold medal. "I knew it. He ate your cattle and threw you in the loch when you attacked him with your sword, and that's when he scratched you. You now have some of his power, and that's why you have lived so long. Can you do anything else?"

"It's a curse, it is. It's far worse than meeting with the devil himself. My family, friends—all gone, even the great-grandchildren of my friends. All gone."

"But you've lived a long time. That's got to be good."

"Nope. It's a curse. I agree it's handy not feeling the cold, and I can swim as good or better than any young man. But I live alone, and local folk think I'm a crazy old man. Years ago, it was different. I was respected."

"They made a movie about you."

"Aye, I heard of such a thing. Probably had some handsome Hollywood actor no doubt playing me, and fools believe it. You kids today have no idea how tough it was. The bloody English were a bunch of murdering maniacs. I worked hard for my money, protecting folks' cattle and my own." Mr. MacGregor ran his finger over the ball of his *shillelagh*, like a parent gently touches a child's hand.

"What type of walking stick is that?"

"It's a *shillelagh*. They are made from a branch of a tree where the handle is the knot. This one is special since it came from a petrified tree."

Archie looked at it and back at Mr. MacGregor. "What was it afraid of?"

"What was afraid?"

"The tree. You said it was petrified."

Mr. MacGregor slowly shook before coughing and bursting out laughing. He was still laughing two minutes later. Archie was annoyed. "Aye, you certainly didn't get any learning done at the school in London you were at." Mr. MacGregor wiped the tears from his eyes.

"Um. What's so funny?"

Mr. MacGregor burst out laughing again until he noticed Archie was frowning. "You're an eejit, Archie. A petrified tree is simply a tree that has been struck by lightning. It makes the wood tougher. The tree itself isn't afraid of anything." He smiled, trying to holding back his laughter.

They were interrupted by a scream from in the village. Both Archie and Mr. MacGregor turned. A woman held her dog's leash, and at the other end, her dog, a fluffy white poodle, was in the grip of a gargoyle. The dog barked and growled, wriggling, trying to get free.

"What in the devil is that beast?" Mr. MacGregor asked.

"A gargoyle. Come on, we have to save the dog." Archie sprinted towards the woman and her dog.

"Are you out of your mind, laddie? Keep away from that thing. It's the devil's doing."

Despite the size of the massive gargoyle, the woman was not about to give up her precious poodle without a fight. The leash snapped. The gargoyle's huge wings flapped, and the gargoyle carried the dog away. Another gargoyle flew down and landed just a few feet from the hysterical woman. It crept towards her slowly, saliva drooling from its mouth as it sized up its next meal.

"Get away! Get away!" Archie shouted.

The woman and the gargoyle simultaneously turned to see a small, half-naked boy with a painted moustache racing towards them. Seeing an easier-sized meal, the gargoyle moved in Archie's direction.

"Get away." Archie stared down the gruesome creature, which stood motionless for a second before reeling backwards in fear. Archie was just a few feet away and could smell the breath of the creature. It reminded him of the time the school toilets blocked up, only ten times worse. The gargoyle let out a squawk, trying to cover its face with its bat-like wings. One flap and it took off into the air, soaring across the village.

The woman fell to her knees crying. "Sodapop. That creature took my little Sodapop."

Archie gently placed his hand on the woman's shoulder. "Are you okay?" Archie asked. "Did it hurt you?"

She looked at him; her tears had made her makeup smudge and run black rivers down her cheeks. She sniffed. "Did you see Sodapop?"

"Sodapop? Is that the name of your dog?" Archie's sweet, unbroken voice brought her back to her senses. She seemed puzzled by his appearance.

"What are you doing out at night half-naked? And what were those monsters? You didn't seem scared. You chased it away." She stood up.

A middle-aged man and woman came over, as they too had heard her screaming.

"Is everything all right?" the man asked.

"No. A creature took my Sodapop."

The couple looked at each other and then at Archie before the man asked another question. "You must be freezing, son. Why would you be eating a sodapop this weather? Is your mom okay?"

"She's not my mom. I heard her scream and came to help."

The woman told them about the monsters and how they stole her Sodapop. Archie thought it best he leave; the couple thought the woman was crazy. He should have informed them that Sodapop was in fact her poodle but thought it best to just leave before they asked too many questions. He quietly said goodbye and left.

His father was working, which gave Archie a few hours to carry out his plan to prevent the nuckelavee from returning. If the sporrans were correct, the nuckelavee would be returning in two days, on Sunday, December 21st.

Archie raced home to collect his swim shorts, a plastic bag, and waterproof flashlight. Archie noticed a long package under the Christmas tree his father had decorated. He picked it up and shook it. A note read: *To Archie, Merry Christmas! Love, Dad.* Archie guessed what it was. He smiled and placed it back under the tree.

He hurried down to the large boulder that had spent thousands of years half-submerged in the loch and half-open to the Scottish elements. The loch's icy waters swallowed him as his dove into its depths. Archie soared through the waters of his new world below the surface. Following the beam from his flashlight, he made his way to the underground cavern. As he broke the water's surface and swam to the edge, a few sporrans came to greet him.

Archie enjoyed visiting them, his own secret little world, safe from gargoyles, school bullies, and memories of his mother. Marlene Bardot walked towards him, her hand on her side, twisting her body in an exaggerated form as if on a model runway walk. She welcomed him in her broken English, her French accent making some words hard to grasp. "Archie, my dear boy, how sweet of you to come back. How nice to see you again. Did I tell you that you are my favorite human?"

"That's because he's the only human you know," Jock said making his way towards Archie. "Besides, how come you are being so nice to him? You must be after something."

Archie climbed out of the water and turned off his flashlight.

"As the only real lady here, I was just being civil. Sophistication probably isn't your strong point, Jock." She gave Jock a sneer and put on a fake smile for Archie. "But since you mentioned it, Archie, I was wondering if it would be possible for you to bring me down a fashion magazine? Miner found one once. It was mostly pictures of ladies in elegant dresses."

"Em. I don't know. My mom used to read them. Full of TV stars and famous people at fancy do's. My dad doesn't read that type of thing. Mostly the paper for soccer news or boating magazines," Archie said, shivering.

"Gordon, you're needed," Jock shouted.

Gordon's long neck rose as he moved snake-like toward Archie. "Let me tell you something. I'm not a hair dryer, you know." He blew hot air over the boy. Archie's hair blew back and was dry in a few seconds.

Archie was unsure how the sporrans would react to the request he was going to make, but just as he was going to speak, Jock came closer and stood next to him. It gave Jock a sense of importance. He felt that Archie was his best friend so that gave him the right to address everyone with Archie. Archie started: "On Sunday, if what you say is true, the nuckelavee will return. The gargoyles are getting braver. Afew people have actually seen them. A farmer told news reporters that two of them flew down and ate his chickens. Of course, everyone thinks he was drunk and don't believe it, but now others are saying similar things.

"A local woman in Foyers had her dog taken while it was still attached to the leash. The gargoyle then went for the woman until I scared it off. That is the second dog I know of they've taken. I think you're right. Foyers and most of the area have more than their fair share. They are gathering here to bring the nuckelavee back to life.

"Gordon, you have to go up and screech or stare at them or whatever it is you do. If not, the gargoyles will resurrect the nuckelavee, and the gargoyles will carry on killing."

Gordon recoiled. "Nuckelavee? I can't fight it! It's not safe for me to surface. The tourists and nuckelavee will see me. No, I won't do it. If the tourists spot me, it will be like it was before. They sent down a submarine and had boats coming and going. Let me tell you something, how am I supposed to catch fish if I hide away?" Steam puffed from his nostrils.

"Okay, calm down, Gordon. Don't get worked up. We will think of something," Llewellyn said.

"I have thought of something," Archie said. "We need to stop the nuckelavee from rising. This way Gordon can do his thing and turn the gargoyles back to stone."

"And how exactly do you propose we do that, Archie? You can't block out the sun or the moon," Marlene Bardot tutted.

"I have a plan but will need the help of a sporran. One of you will have to come up to the surface with me," Archie said.

The sporrans all took a few steps back. Jock started to slowly shuffle away from Archie and join the others.

"The surface?" Marlene Bardot asked, her eyes open wide like she had seen a gargoyle. "Are you ding-a-ling? That would be a suicide mission in normal circumstances, but if you are right about the gargoyles grouping together around Loch Ness, then it would be *folle*."

"*Folle*?" Archie asked.

"It's French for, how you say," she paused. "Crazy!"

Archie was disappointed when he noticed Jock had moved further away from him.

"Let me tell you something, Archie. What you ask is too much. The gargoyles would sniff out a sporran and take one as a snack," Gordon said.

Archie ran his fingers through his hair and sighed heavily.

"If none of you are prepared to do anything, I don't know why I bothered to come down. You are as bad as Evan and his friends. You tell me all this stuff about gargoyles and a nuckelavee, and then do nothing to help. I'm ten. What am I supposed to do?"

"I thought you were ten-and-a-half?" Gordon joked.

Some of the sporrans laughed. Archie looked upset. He picked up his flashlight and turned to go back to the water's edge.

"That's it? You're leaving?" Marlene Bardot asked.

Archie turned. "I've had enough of people laughing at me tonight." A single tear rolled down his cheek.

The pitiful site of his new friend being upset was enough for Jock to slowly move forward. "Archie," he paused, taking a breath. "Archie, I'll do it."

The sporrans gasped. Archie smiled at him and picked him up.

"How long can you hold your breath for?" Archie asked.

Jock said nothing but started to shake.

Gordon's massive head swung down to Archie. "Take care of him Archie and . . ." Gordon hesitated before continuing. "Be careful. You may think you can scare off a gargoyle with your powers, but you may not be strong enough to handle a whole gaggle of them."

"So will you help?" Archie asked.

Gordon recoiled and whined in a high pitch voice. "But the nuckelavee. It might wake up."

Archie placed Jock in the plastic bag. He tied the top and ran back into the water, and after taking a deep breath, he dove into the underground lake and followed it back out to the entrance to the loch. For the entire journey back to the surface and Archie's home, Jock kept his eyes closed, terrified of what he might see.

# Chapter Twenty-One

"Where are we?" Jock asked when he finally opened his eyes.

"This is my bedroom." Archie rubbed his hair dry with a towel.

"What's that smell?" Jock asked.

"Oh, that's you. I put some of my dad's cologne on you so the gargoyles won't be able to smell you."

Jock held his little hands up to the center of his body, just below his eyes.

"Do you have a nose?" Archie asked.

"Not like that great big thing sticking out of your face. Sporrans have scent glands. Much better, if you ask me. Can I see the television? I've never seen one before."

Archie carried Jock downstairs, turned the TV on, and tenderly put Jock on the couch to watch it.

"Yellow people. Why are they yellow? And that one has blue hair!"

Archie laughed and sat down next to him. "They're not real. They're cartoons, and that's *The Simpsons*. It's a funny show."

Jock enjoyed himself with Archie. He had so many questions about the boy's home, such as why he had a tree with lights in the home. What made the flames work in the gas fire? Why did Archie sleep in a different room from his father? Sporrans all lived together, so it seemed strange that humans would sleep shut in different rooms from the people they loved.

Archie sat with Jock watching TV and eating tangerines, although Jock thought the peel was much tastier than the actual flesh.

*

Throughout Scotland, gargoyles converged, mostly around Loch Ness, hidden in trees and up on rooftops. Archie's father went to the school to collect his son from the dance. He noticed the children leaving were not wearing fancy dress, so he rushed into the school looking for Archie. He found Chloe. She informed him that Evan had tricked Archie, and how he had run off upset. He cursed under his breath and left in a hurry to find his son.

When the door handle rattled, Archie scooped up Jock and shoved him up his shirt.

"Archie! Are you okay? Chloe told me what happened. Just wait until I see that Evan. I'll be giving him a piece of my mind." His father sat down next to Archie and ruffled his hair.

"I'm fine *now*. It was embarrassing, and I bet they laugh and say stuff at school about it."

After a few minutes of watching TV, Archie made an excuse that he was tired, said goodnight, and went up to his room. He pulled Jock out from his place of hiding.

"It's hotter than Gordon's breath under there," Jock complained.

"Sorry, I couldn't let my dad see you. Well, not until tomorrow when the whole town will see you." Archie pulled on his pajamas.

Jocks eyes opened wide, and his mouth dropped. "The whole town? Not the whole town of humans?"

"Just close your eyes and keep your mouth closed, and they will assume you are just a sporran," Archie said reassuringly.

"*Just* a sporran. I'm Jock Sporran, a true Scottish sporran from a long line of sporrans before me. My family has lived here for thousands of years. Not like Marlene Bardot, who came from France, and Llewellyn and Miner who came from Wales. They came from all over the world to seek protection from Gordon. My family was already here, so I'm not *just* a sporran, Archie."

"I didn't mean it like that. I meant they will think you are just like everyone else's fake sporran. Only you and I will know the truth," Archie said, brushing his fingers over Jock's head.

"What's our plan?" Jock asked.

Archie turned out the light and climbed into bed. Jock sat on his pillow.

"Maybe it will be better that you don't know. It's gonna be scary. I just wish Gordon would help," Archie said before putting on a deep voice mimicking Gordon. *"Let me tell you something."*

"Gordon would fry you if he heard you doing that," Jock chuckled. "He may be a sea dragon who can breathe fire and turn gargoyles to stone with his stare or roar, but he's a coward."

"I know. Good night." Archie yawned.

"How long will you be sleeping for?" Jock asked.

Archie lifted himself onto his elbow and looked at the tiny fluffy figure sat on his pillow. "Um, I will wake up about eight I guess, so about ten hours. How long do you sleep for?"

"Sporrans don't sleep. We rest, close our eyes, but never sleep."

Archie laid his head back down on the pillow. Within a few minutes, Jock was fascinated watching Archie's chest rise and fall while he slept. Jock snuggled in close to Archie's neck, listening to his human friend breathing heavy while he slept.

After an hour passed, Jock sat up and climbed up onto the headboard and made his way to the windowsill. He marveled the view of the loch at night. The full moon lit up the entire area. Suddenly he noticed a dark figure flying in the sky, then another, and another, followed by more.

It was the first time Jock had seen a gargoyle, and now he was witnessing any sporran's worst nightmare. Hundreds of gargoyles were flying above the loch, some on the bank and some in the trees, and even some on the roof of Archie's cottage. Suddenly the bedroom door opened and a dark figure appeared.

Jock froze, afraid to move a muscle. He opened his mouth to call Archie but nothing came out. The tall figure made its way to Archie's bed. Jock felt helpless as he watched the figure bend down towards Archie. Jock stood up; he was going to pounce and save his friend. Just as he was about to jump he noticed the large figure push his lips on Archie's cheek. The large dark figure pulled the covers up to Archie's shoulders.

Jock guessed that it was Archie's father and that the lips touching Archie's face was what Marlene Bardot called a kiss. It was the first time Jock had seen a full-size human. From stories, he had heard how they captured sporrans, used the skins to make purses, and stuffed the rest to make a haggis. Jock was surprised to see how lovingly they could be towards each other.

When Archie's father left the room, closing the door behind him, Jock watched out the window again. To his horror, he saw dozens of gargoyles flying across the sky, some landing on rooftops and trees. One flew close and actually peered in the window as it flew past. It was grotesque, with the body of an ape with wings and its head half-lion, half-serpent.

Jock climbed back down to Archie's bed and snuggled against Archie's neck. It was warm, and much safer than looking out the window.

## Chapter Twenty-Two

Imran Akran, his parents, and his older brother had driven the previous day from London to Glasgow. This morning, they were driving to Foyers and would be staying at the White Stag Inn for two days. They had brought a Christmas present for Archie and wanted to surprise him.

Archie hadn't seen Imran since he left London. Mrs. Akran knew that Archie's first Christmas without his mother would be difficult and wanted to find out how he was settling in. She hoped seeing Imran again would cheer him up a little just before Christmas.

Imran's older brother wanted to see Scotland, as well, so the Akran family chose to spend a few days in Scotland just before Christmas and surprise Archie. Mrs. Akran had told Archie's father when they would be arriving. He kept it a secret from Archie. He had briefly met Mrs. Akran when he first met Archie.

*

Archie was woken by a thud and something shouting, "Ouch!" He rolled to the edge of his bed and looked down on the floor. Jock sat on the floor rubbing his head.

"What did you do that for?" Jock complained.

"Oh sorry! Did I kick you out of bed?" Archie yawned.

"I spent all night guarding you and that's the thanks I get?" Jock dusted himself off.

Archie jumped out of bed, scooped Jock up, and took him to the bathroom. He placed Jock on the edge of the sink.

"Well, close your eyes. I need to pee," Archie said.

Jock looked away while Archie took care of his business. When the toilet flushed, Jock looked around the room.

"Oh, so that's where you go," Jock said.

Archie smeared toothpaste on his brush. "Yeah were else do you think we go?"

"I didn't know. I needed to go last night and um . . ." Jock looked guilty. "Well, I wasn't sure where to go . . . so I used one of your shoes."

Archie stared at Jock, his mouth full of frothy white toothpaste. "You used my shoe as a toilet?" Archie said, spitting toothpaste over Jock.

"Yeah. Sorry. Stop spitting that white stuff on me!"

Archie finished brushing his teeth and collected his shoes. He came back into the bathroom holding his nose.

"That's gross. I can't believe you took a dump in my shoe. Ew, it's green, slimy, and it stinks!" Archie held his nose with one hand and tipped the offending mess out of his shoe and down the toilet. "What have you been eating that smells like something dead?"

"I normally eat just potatoes, carrots, and parsnips. I think it must have been the tangerine peel you gave me."

Archie wiped out his shoe and cleaned it out under the water. "Just don't do it in my shoes again. I have to wear them to church today."

A knock at the bathroom door made Archie and Jock jump.

"Morning. Are you okay in there, Archie?" his father asked. "I made breakfast."

"Yes, Dad, I'm just coming."

After breakfast, Archie went back to his room with a carrot for Jock to eat, which Jock ate watching Archie get dressed into his kilt.

Archie admired himself in the mirror before picking Jock up. "I can either clip you to my belt or you can hang on with your hands."

"You're not clipping me to nothing. I can hold on." With his tiny hands, Jock grabbed the belt that held up Archie's kilt.

Archie looked at himself again in the mirror and tucked his shirt in. "I look like a girl in this kilt."

Jock opened an eye and peeked at himself and Archie. "You look like a fine Scot, Archie. And if I say so myself, I look quite handsome . . . in a fluffy kind of way."

"Keep your eyes closed, and whatever you do, don't let your legs down," Archie ordered.

Archie walked downstairs, where he found his father adjusting his own kilt. "Archie, boy, you look great. Let me take a good look." He stood back and took a good look at his son.

"I feel weird in this kilt," Archie said, frowning.

"Nonsense, you look like a true Scotsman. And where did you get the sporran from? It looks new."

"I borrowed it from a friend, " Archie said.

"*It?* Who are you calling *it*?" Jock hissed.

His father looked at Archie. "Did you say something?"

"Um. I said we had better *get*. We don't want to be late. It's seven-thirty," Archie said, putting his hand over Jock's mouth. "Um, Dad?" Archie paused. "You may not be that proud of me. I think I broke a Scottish rule."

His father looked down at him and raised his eyebrows. "Well, spit it out, son. What've you done?"

"Well, it's cold out. And I know I read that Scottish men don't wear underwear under their kilts. As I'm only half-Scottish, I wore mine." Archie gave a tight-lipped smile.

His father laughed and rubbed Archie's hair. "Ha! That's an old Scot's tale. Just like they say we eat porridge with salt on it. Yuck. Of course we wear underwear under our kilts. It's cleaner, warmer, and on a windy day, decent. I doubt anyone goes commando under a kilt nowadays, son."

\*

Foyers Church was traditionally a Protestant church, but times had changed. The community had adapted and welcomed all—Protestants, Catholics, Jews, Muslims and even non-believers attended. It was more a traditional gathering of local people. This time of year, the men and boys braved the icy weather and wore kilts with white shirts and tartan jackets. The women and girls wore tartan skirts and dresses with matching bonnets. As for the church service, it was usually relaxed. They sang a selection of Christmas carols. Often, children from the local early learning center performed a nativity play. Some Muslim children told a story of Jesus's mother, Mary, and some Jewish children read the story of Hanukkah. A tiny group of non-believing children spoke about Christmas, and how it is a good time of the year to give to others.

When he and his father approached the church, Archie felt at ease seeing the men and boys of all ages wearing kilts. He licked his finger to find the wind's direction before he noticed Evan and his friends. Archie decided to keep well away from them in the future. The moon was still visible in the sky at the far end of the loch. Archie knew, in a few minutes, the sun would be rising at the other end. He hoped his plan would work.

It was no warmer inside the church, and any heat from the small electric fires mounted on the four pillars went straight into the high ceilings.

"Dad, I want to sit with Chloe. Is that okay?" Archie asked and, before waiting for an answer, disappeared along a pew, leaving his father to sit with other locals.

The church soon filled. The organist played strange versions of Christmas carols while everyone arrived and got seated. Every seat was taken, and a few had to stand at the back of the church. In the hustle, Archie slipped out the back door.

Once outside, after checking the coast was clear, he ran around the side of the church and was about to head home when he noticed a gargoyle fly from a nearby yew tree to the church roof. It was followed by two others.

"Uh oh. Gargoyles are everywhere," Archie said as he ran.

Jock held on tight. He was getting bounced around hanging onto Archie's belt and kept his eyes shut. "Okay, I'll say it. I'm scared, Archie."

"We just have to do this."

"If I get scared half-to-death twice, does that mean I'm dead?"

"Don't worry, Jock. I'm with you. The only time you can be brave is when you are afraid, and right now, we have to be brave."

As Archie got closer to his home, it was evident that the gargoyles had started to settle. Archie's exceptional vision gave him an advantage, and he could see them hiding in trees. Some braver gargoyles had actually started to stand on the rugged bank of the loch.

With all the local villagers in church, no one could see them. The gargoyles didn't care for any moment. Now the morning sun would raise enough, and the nuckelavee would resurrect from death itself.

Archie burst into the front door and slammed it shut behind him. "Okay. You can open your eyes. We are home now."

Jock opened his eyes and dropped to the ground.

"Thank goodness that is over. I was scared to death. There were humans everywhere. Fat ones. Thin ones. Some tall, short, black, white, boys, girls, men, and women."

"It's not over yet. The worst is yet to come, so I need you to be brave, Jock," Archie ripped open his large Christmas present.

"It may not be over, but it's not Christmas yet, Archie. You can't open your presents now. Besides it's bad luck," Jock said.

Archie ignored him and ripped the Christmas paper from the box. He opened the box and smiled.

"Parents are so predictable."

"What is it?"

"It's my Christmas present. A dual-line stunt kite."

"Archie, have you lost your mind? There are hundreds of gargoyles out there. The nuckelavee is about to be resurrected and you are playing with a kite?"

Undeterred, Archie knelt on the floor, and with his tongue resting on the side of his mouth, he assembled the kite. The sturdy red kite had a long yellow tail made of ribbon. He attached the two cords and looked at his watch. It was almost nine o'clock. If Llewellyn was correct, the sun and moon would be at the precise location in twelve minutes and twelve seconds.

"Okay, it's ready, Jock," Archie said, looking out the window. "I need you to be brave and . . ." Archie voice trailed off. He cursed, staring out the window.

"Did you say what I think you said, Archie?" Jock smiled. "I don't know much about humans, but I know humans who are only ten should not be using words like that."

Archie couldn't believe his eyes. Hundreds of gargoyles lined the banks of Loch Ness. They came in all sizes, each one as grotesque and ugly as the next. He gulped, took a deep breath, and picked up Jock.

"What's the plan, Archie? And just how dangerous is this going to be?" Jock asked.

Archie carried him over to the sink. He turned on the water and washed Jock under the flowing water, ignoring his protests.

"Agh! Stop it! It's cold! Are you crazy? I'm soaked now. Why are you doing this? I thought we were friends?" Jock spluttered.

Archie wrapped him in a towel and rubbed him dry.

"Sorry, Jock. I had to wash off the cologne."

"Oh, well a bit of warning would have been nice. Won't the gargoyles be able to smell my scent now?"

"Yes, that is the whole idea. According to Marlene Bardot, gargoyles love eating sporrans and can detect one from miles away."

Archie tied the yellow ribbon tail from the kite around Jock. "You will have to hang on tight as well. I don't want it too tight, or it will hurt. So, hang on."

Jock looked at the ribbon tied around his middle. "What are you gonna do Archie? I don't like it. I'm getting really scared now! I'm doomed!"

Archie lifted Jock and kissed him. "Trust me, Jock. I won't let anyone hurt you. Just hang on tight and leave the rest to me." Archie looked at his watch again.

"I'm doomed! *Doomed*!"

"No, you're not."

"But I'm scared, Archie."

"The wind is perfect. Lets go now."

*

Inside the church the locals sang carol after carol before the nativity play started. The entire village was deeply engrossed in the Christmas service.

*

Archie picked up the kite, left the cottage, and looked up at the heavens. Lightning reined in the sky, sizzling and crackling, zigzagging from sky to ground. Archie had seen lightning before but only when it had been cloudy and raining. A loud thunderclap followed and echoed across the loch, shaking the ground and stimulating the water.

Archie proceeded to the loch. His normally smiling mouth was a grim slash of determination. He had one chance. He would allow nothing to break his concentration. He had to block out the light from the sun and moon.

No sooner had they ventured outside then Jock's scent was picked up by the closest of the gargoyles. They growled, licked their wart-covered lips, and turned to see where the delicious scent was coming from. A particularly ghastly gargoyle, who was hunched over no more than fifty feet away on the edge of the loch, slowly raised its hideous head. Its snot-dripping, grisly nostrils sniffed at the air. As if in slow-motion, its eyes looked left in Archie's direction. The horrific monstrous creature's lips curled back, exposing black, decaying, ferocious fangs.

"Archie . . . the gargoyles . . . they're coming!"

"Hang on tight," Archie said, laying the kite and Jock on the ground. He walked backwards, unraveling the strings.

Jock, paralyzed with fear, hung on tight to the ribbon. "I'm doomed!"

The gargoyle flapped its wings and took off, coming straight at Archie and Jock, its snake-like tongue dripping with anticipation of a fresh meal of human boy and the favorite delicacy of live sporran.

As it approached, Archie turned and glared at it. Nothing happened. It was still coming. Jock was petrified. Archie doubted he could scare it away in time. The gargoyle gave a spine-tingling squawk. It flapped and hovered in midair, taunted by the presence of a meal and the orange eyes of the boy.

Archie kept walking backwards uncoiling the strings to the kite while keeping his eyes on the gargoyle. All his work of the past three days had led to this moment. With a quick jerk, he hailed the kite up into the sky, which was followed by the tail of the kite and Jock, tied on tight.

"Aah," Jock cried. "Archie, are you crazeeeeeeee?"

Archie continued to unravel the strings wound around two plastic handles. The kite flew higher and higher until the full force of the wind took it up over the loch. He had taken his eyes off the gargoyle and was concentrating on the kite. The scent of live sporran carried with the wind across the entire length of Loch Ness. The gargoyles growled, and took to the sky. Hundreds of the loathsome creatures headed towards the kite. Archie checked his watch. He had a little under a minute to go before the nuckelavee would rise from the depths. The icy waters of Loch Ness crashed violently against the jagged shoreline. Archie stood on the outcropping rock, fighting with the kite, his tongue pocking out to the side of his mouth as he concentrated on keeping the kite and Jock airborne and safe.

## Chapter Twenty-Three

A smaller, faster gargoyle that looked half-eagle half-mountain lion got close to Jock and snapped its mouth at him. Archie anticipated it and tugged hard on the right cord, sending the kite plummeting. As it headed towards the surface of the water, Archie pulled left and then on both cords, sending the kite soaring up into the sky.

A huge flock of screeching gargoyles had gathered chase, many crashing into each other, all trying to catch the sporran. Archie walked towards the edge of the rock, uncoiled more cord, and let the kite higher. Another attack from both sides came at the kite. At least forty gargoyles gave chase. Archie pushed forward with his right hand and pulled back with his left. The kite spun in circles towards the water's surface once more. As it approached the surface, Archie let it run along a few feet above the water, causing a few gargoyles to slam into the water.

Another glance at his watch. It was almost time. He pulled back on both strings and sent the kite high into the sky once more. Over four hundred gargoyles, now airborne, chased the kite, many of them dwarfing the red plastic toy with its yellow tail. Jock held on tight, keeping his eyes closed throughout, terrified of being high in the sky chased by hundreds of bloodthirsty gargoyles.

Two large, clawed feet kicked Archie to the ground. He fell flat on his face, almost falling into the loch, but still hanging on tightly to the cords. The same gargoyle attacked him again, pinning him facedown on the ground. The kite flew stationary. Gargoyles fought each other to take a bite at the sporran.

The gargoyle pinning Archie down opened its huge mouth and took aim at the back of the boy's neck.

"Be gone with ya," a Scottish voice shouted. The gargoyle turned to see old Mr. MacGregor hobbling towards them. His orange eyes glared at the gargoyle, as he waved his *shillelagh* at the creature.

It jumped off Archie and retreated, hissing and squawking wildly at the man. Archie climbed to his knees and pulled back on the string. The wind had increased as he struggled with the kite.

"What do you have tied on the kite?" Mr. MacGregor shouted above the noise of the wind and squawks of the gargoyles.

"A sporran."

"The daft creatures must think it's real."

"It is." Archie pulled back on the left string, avoiding another attack on the kite.

"I heard about them when I was a lad, but thought it was just a myth." Mr. MacGregor looked at the gargoyles in the sky.

The time had come. It was twelve minutes and twelve seconds after nine o'clock. The sky was full of gargoyles, and as the sun and moon elevated together, the loch remained dark. The moon and sun were blocked by a massive wall of flapping, abominable gargoyles. The very creatures that had come to raise the nuckelavee were, in fact, blocking the light.

Another gargoyle came in to attack, but MacGregor stared it out. It was soon replaced by another and another, each one getting braver by the second. Mr. MacGregor waved his *shillelagh* and tried to shoo them away. The gargoyles appeared to be scared of him. His eyes and the boy's had the orange tint, but in their sheer numbers, it was possible they could defeat the boy and old man.

As they got closer, Mr. MacGregor smashed them with his *shillelagh*. Desperation drove Mr. MacGregor to fight on. It had been over 250 years since he had needed to fight like this. His body complained, and he felt the tearing of his shoulder muscles, the weakness of paralysis seeping through him like rigor mortis. But he obstinately resisted the urge to fall, and kept swinging, kept pounding with his *shillelagh* and kicking his foot at them.

*

The Akran family car turned a final corner, giving them their first view of Loch Ness, although today, the sky was filled with hundreds of gargoyles. Mr. Akran stopped the car in disbelief. Imran pressed his face against the window and peered out. "What is this place? Jurassic Park?"

After a few minutes, the family continued their journey into Foyers. The village was deserted. Inside the church, the villagers were triumphantly singing at the top of their voices along with the massive church organ "Silent Night." Outside the church there was anything but silence. The flapping of large heavy wings and squawks of the gargoyles carried on the wind.

"Look. There's someone," Mr. Akran said pointing at Mr. MacGregor. "And he's with that girl flying a kite. Those creatures seem to be attacking her kite . . . no . . . it's a boy in a kilt!"

"That looks like Archie," Imran's older brother Muhammad said.

The family car got closer.

"It *is* Archie," Imran said excitedly.

Mr. MacGregor felled a gargoyle who was swooping down with claws and fangs at the ready. With seconds to spare, Mr. MacGregor looked up and stared at the creature. "Be away with you!" he shouted, waving his arms and breathing heavily as he struggled to climb to his feet.

More gargoyles swopped down; the constant squawking was deafening. The moon rays were blocked by the mass of gargoyles, but it seemed Archie's plan had worked for now. Yet the scent of Jock had driven them into a frenzy.

Mr. Akran stopped the car on the side of the road, the family staring wide-eyed at the scene before them. Hundreds of gargoyles circled the sky, attacking a kite that Archie controlled, and as some gargoyles tried to attack Archie, the old man with the huge grey sideburns stared them down and wove his stick as if it was a sword.

"It's been years since I had so much fun," Mr. MacGregor shouted to Archie while waving his *shillelagh*. "These beasts are as relentless as the English."

Imran unclipped his seat belt and opened the back door of the car and ran towards Archie.

"Imran, get back in!" his mother shrieked.

A gargoyle landed on the roof of the car. Imran's brother pulled the door shut. Another gargoyle landed on the windshield, its claws scrapping across the glass. It shrieked at the car's occupants.

"Archie! Archie Wilson!" Imran hollered, running towards his friend with a huge smile on his face.

A gargoyle snapped at the kite and ripped a small hole in the edge. It was too close for comfort. Archie had to concentrate, as Jock was now in severe danger.

"Archie Wilson!" Imran shouted again, running towards him.

Archie's newly improved senses picked up the sound. The familiar voice from his friend finally registered. Archie turned his head and couldn't believe his eyes. His best friend Imran was running towards him and just a few feet above him, swooping down close, was a massive gargoyle, its jaws open, displaying a huge set of fangs.

Archie had to think quickly. If he let go of the kite strings. it would fall into the loch and Jock would possibly drown. That was *if* a gargoyle didn't catch him on the way down. If he ignored Imran, the gargoyle zooming in on him would soon have him in his clutches. With no time for second-guessing, Archie did the unthinkable and dropped the strings and raced towards Imran. He leaped off the boulder and ran up the grass bank. The kite and Jock started to dive down, chased by at least sixty gargoyles.

"Get away! Go! Shoo!" Archie shouted at the gargoyle chasing Imran. It was too late. It grasped the collar of Imran's shirt in its claws and lifted the boy from the ground. Archie dived at him and caught hold of Imran's legs. The extra weight ripped Imran's shirt collar free, and Imran and Archie fell on the ground. Archie stood and faced the gargoyle. It shrieked at him, flapping wildly.

More gargoyles attacked the car, cracking the windshield. A tire was ripped open by the jaws of a gargoyle. Others pounded on the roof. Archie may have stopped the nuckelavee but at high cost.

"Are you okay?" Archie asked.

"That was wicked! This place is awesome!" Imran beamed, clearly not understanding the danger he was in.

Jock crashed down into the water and almost immediately started to go down. His silky fur absorbed the water and the weight pulled him down. Further along the loch, the water churned. The sun and moonlight blocked out by the gargoyles made the loch's water look black. A churning black soup of water erupted, followed by a mighty roar.

Gordon had been watching from just below the surface and couldn't ignore it anymore. Archie and Jock were in serious trouble, and only he could save his friends. He surfaced from the depths and spewed out a massive flame that shot out over sixty feet across the sky. His roar was deafening and was travelled on the wind. He swam along the loch, roaring up at the sky. Gargoyles instantly turned back into stone and came crashing down on the loch.

With Imran out of danger, Archie ran back towards the loch, dodging the stone gargoyles that rained down. He dove into the water and swam as fast as he could to the area where the kite had come down. It was a long swim. Archie gritted his teeth and powered on, giving it everything he had, swimming as fast as he could, using everything he had learned from swimming lessons—long stroke, fingers closed like a paddle, and head down. Every now and then a gargoyle that had been turned to stone by Gordon's growl came crashing down into the water, just missing Archie. He came to the kite, but he faced his biggest dread. Jock was gone. Taking a deep breath, Archie dove below the surface, frantically searching for Jock. Deeper and deeper he swam, his eyes growing accustomed to the darkness. *Had Jock been caught and eaten by a gargoyle? No,* Archie told himself. The thought was too terrible to imagine. Archie swam deeper until he noticed a few tiny air bubbles rising. He swam harder and discovered Jock, lifeless, sinking. Archie caught Jock and immediately headed back to the surface, dodging the stone gargoyles crushing down into the water.

Archie's head broke the water's surface, and he lifted Jock up out of the water. The wet sporran was limp, his little pink arms and legs swinging lifelessly.

"Jock. Jock speak to me," Archie pleaded, swimming with one arm back to shore.

Gordon dove deep and came up at full speed. He breached the surface as his entire body left the water. He gave a large growl before plummeting back into the depths. It had been years since he had breached. For seventy years since the last time someone had seen him, tourists gathered hoping to catch a glimpse.

Mr. Akran opened the door to his car and ran down the grass bank and helped Imran to his feet.

"Are you hurt, my son?" Mr. Akran asked in his Pakistani accent.

"Wow! That was the bomb. Can I get an "Amen!"? Was that the Loch Ness Monster?" Imran asked, looking out at the loch with a huge grin on his face. Mrs. Akran and Muhammad joined them.

"Our car is a wreck, Dad," Muhammad said, looking back at the car that barely survived the attack from gargoyles. One had turned to stone on the roof, making it seem like they had picked it up from a garden center to take home as a yard ornament.

"Are you okay, laddie?" Mr. MacGregor asked.

"Yes, sir, but where's Archie? He can't swim very far."

They looked out into the waters of the loch. Archie was swimming back with one arm, clutching Jock with the other. They helped Archie out of the water. He was unconcerned about the cold. He tried to gently shake Jock back to life. Archie was on his knees with the wet furry creature on its back in front of him. He bent down and kissed him. "Jock. Wake up, Jock. We got to take you home. We did it, Jock." Archie looked up at Mrs. Akran with tears flooding from his eyes. "Mrs. Akran, wake him up. Tell him it's gonna be okay now. We did it." Archie sobbed, rubbing Jock.

The Akran family was not sure what to say. Archie was beside himself with grief over what they could only see was a soft cuddly toy. "Jock. Wake up. Wake up, Jock," Archie cried, placing his head on Jock. It was a pitiful sight. A young boy, soaking wet, was sitting in a freezing cold wind, crying over a wet, lifeless creature.

"The beast is coming back," Mr. MacGregor shouted.

Gordon was heading towards them. Within a few seconds he was on the edge of the bank. He stretched his long neck and looked down at them huddled around Archie.

"Be away with ya," Mr. MacGregor shouted, waving his *shillelagh* at Gordon.

"Oh, puh-lease," Gordon said. "What exactly is that going to do to me?"

Mr. MacGregor and the Akran family all looked on in amazement. Before them, not only stood the Loch Ness Monster, but it spoke to them.

"Get away I'll not tell you again," MacGregor shouted at Gordon.

## Chapter Twenty-Four

Darkness spread across the sky. The wind stopped, and everything went silent. Gordon pulled his head away, his eyes darting left and right up and down the loch. There was something else. Archie was aware of an approaching blackness, a sense of something so terrifying that he was almost afraid to look.

No more than fifty feet away, the water bubbled and boiled. Steam rose from the water, and from the steam, a figure appeared—a dark, silent creature. It looked like a horse with a legless rider perched on its back, although the rider seemed to be part of the horse. There was an engaging clumsiness about the creature as it plodded out of the water. The head of the rider was ten times larger than a human head. It had a large mouth that jutted out like a pig's snout. It had one large red eye that was a glowing flame. It finally walked onto the bank. This was when they noticed the horse's hooves where actually feet with claws.

Gordon dove under the water.

"This place is way better than Jurassic Park," Imran beamed.

"Oh, sweet mother of Jesus, are we in trouble now," Mr. MacGregor said. "It's a . . ." He could hardly bring himself to say it.

Archie looked up through tear-soaked eyes. "The nuckelavee." All strength and blood seemed suddenly to have been drained from his body. At last he knew, as he had never known before, the fear of the unknown that haunted thousands before him. His every limb trembled, and his head swam. It was hard to focus.

The creature looked around at its surroundings. Stone gargoyles were everywhere. Its one eye focused on the group on the water's edge. As it slowly walked towards them, the grass around the creature turned black as if it was burnt, leaving a trail of dead and burnt foliage. A diabolical howl bellowed from its mouth, louder than anything they had heard before.

"Please, tell me someone is catching this on a camera?" Imran said. "It will go viral."

As the nuckelavee got closer, Mr. MacGregor walked in front of them. "Get behind me."

The nuckelavee was something like Archie had never seen before. Everything the sporrans had told him was true, but it was far more menacing. The gruesome creature approaching him was the most cruel and malignant of all the uncanny beings that trouble mankind. The lower part of this terrible monster was like a great horse, with flappers like fins about his legs. Its mouth as wide as a shark, from which came breath like steam from a kettle.

On him sat, or rather seemed to grow from his back, a huge man with no legs, and ape-like arms that reached nearly to the ground. His huge head kept rolling from one shoulder to the other as if it was about to tumble off.

But what was most horrible of all was that the monster was skinless—this utter want of skin adding much to the terrific appearance of the creature's naked body. The whole surface of it showed red raw flesh, in which Archie saw blood, dark red as cherry, running through translucent veins, and great white muscles, twisting and contracting as the nuckelavee moved.

Archie and the others were terrified, their hair on end, a cold sensation like a film of ice between their scalps and brains, and a cold sweat bursting from every pore. At the same time, an earsplitting scream echoed all around them.

Pain followed like no headache before. So much pressure built up, everyone thought the veins in their temples would burst. Mr. MacGregor fell to his knees. Imran was the first to cry out in pain.

He collapsed on the ground holding his head. His brother and parents followed. Archie and Mr. MacGregor were next. It was as if the nuckelavee had forced them to bow before him before he killed them. Archie clung to the ground, which seemed to be getting hotter as if hell itself was about to erupt.

The Nuckelavee gave another howl that carried across the loch like thunder. It approached the humans and opened its massive mouth. Its breath turned the nearby evergreen tree leaves brown.

The nuckelavee had been resurrected and stood before them ready to take over. Archie's plan had failed, and before him were the nuckelavee's first victims. The beast never noticed the small movement next to Archie; it was too intent on killing the humans. Jock had miraculously recovered and slowly climbed to his feet. "Hey you big Jessy. Be gone with you and your nasty mingin breath and leave Archie Wilson alone," Jock shouted.

The nuckelavee reared up, trying to back away, and gave an ear-piercing screech, followed by a howl as loud as thunder, all aimed at Jock. It backed away, as Jock faced him.

"I said be gone, you spawny-eyed pig-faced wazzock," Jock shouted brushing himself off, knowing his tiny hair would hurt the creature.

The pain in Archie's head subsided as he looked up in astonishment. Jock was not only alive, but he was scaring away the nuckelavee and calling it names. The nuckelavee backed away in fear, screaming and howling at the sporran. Archie climbed to his feet, sticking close behind Jock. He picked up Mr. MacGregor's *shillelagh* and, with all his strength, threw it at the nuckelavee like a spear. It stuck into the body of the creature, wedged between its rib bones.

Giving a mighty howl, the horse stamped around while the creature on its back tried to remove the wooden *shillelagh*. As it struggled and howled in pain, Gordon surfaced from the depths and, with a mighty roar, bellowed out a huge ball of fire at the nuckelavee, carpeting it in flames. The petrified wood of the *shillelagh* caught on fire, and the nuckelavee was engulfed in flames. Foiled by its intended victim and screaming in pain, it collapsed in on itself. Thick black smoke bellowed towards the sky. In a matter of moments, a pile of smoldering ash lay where the nuckelavee stood. Gordon roared again, a huge flume of fire scattering the ashes into the wind. Just for good measure and feeling pleased with himself, Gordon gave a mighty roar, shattering windows from nearby homes. The nuckelavee was dead.

As a team, Jock, Archie, and Gordon had defeated the nuckelavee, although Gordon later confessed in confidence to Archie he was terrified and said the event probably put decades on him.

Imran and his family climbed to their feet and helped Mr. MacGregor up. Archie approached Jock, bent down, picked him up, and kissed him.

"Ugh! That's so gross," Jock complained. "Boys don't kiss boys."

"I thought I lost you, I thought you drowned. I'm sorry I had to let the kite go to save Imran and . . ." Archie fought back the tears.

"Archie, this place is wicked, and that fluffy thing talks too, and those two monsters were epic, and the gargoyles . . . This is place teracool. Did you see the flames from the dragon thing?" Imran was unable to hold back his excitement, unable to grasp that he and his entire family were almost killed.

That was when Archie realized for the first time that he and Imran had grown apart. For now, Archie was more mature. He had saved Chloe and Imran from a gargoyle. His actions saved Scotland—and maybe even lands further afield—from disaster. Imran was still the same ten-year-old boy Archie had left behind in London. Archie had outgrown that life; he was now part of Foyers and part of Loch Ness.

The most important thing now was trying to at act as if nothing happened. If news of this broke, then the secret life of the sporrans and Gordon would be at risk and even Archie himself with his newfound strength and powers could be at risk.

## Chapter Twenty-Five

The church service finished, and the congregation slowly started to walk out into the cold Scottish air. It would be several hours later when some started to discover concrete gargoyles on their rooftops they didn't remember seeing before. The broken windows were put down to a freak-of-nature gust of wind.

Imran Akran and his family were a problem Archie had to deal with. They stood around the family car as Mr. Akran removed the luggage from the trunk. "I am wondering what the insurance man is saying when he sees this," Mr. Akran said. "Oh, goodness gracious me. He isn't going to be happy. But there's an old Hindu saying that says, 'Always turn a disaster into an opportunity.'"

"But, Dad . . . the car's toast." Imran kicked the tire a huge gargoyle had taken a bite out of.

"That is why I pay the insurance man. We will be driving a new car, and we are all well," Mr. Akran said.

"Yeah and I guess once we tell all the newspapers and TV, we will be famous," Muhammad said.

Archie walked forward. "Um . . . there probably won't be any newspapers or TV. It's best we say nothing."

"Have you bumped your head, Archie? How can you say that? This is dinosaurland and you have the fluffy thing that talks!" Imran said.

"This is a sporran." Archie said.

"Exactly. I bet it's rare, and all the nature shows will want to film it."

"There we go again with the *it* thing," Jock snapped. "Why do humans call me *it*?"

"The reason he's alive is because he's not on TV," Archie said. "If people found out about one of the world's rarest creatures they would stick him in a zoo for people to stare at and poke fun at." Archie was annoyed. "Imran, you can't want that for him. He's my friend, and if any of you tell anyone about what you saw today, his life is over. This whole village would be full of tourists from all over the globe."

Mrs. Akran nodded and smiled. "Archie Wilson, you have changed and certainly grown up in such a short time." She looked at her sons. "Archie is right. We can't say anything. Whatever these creatures are, they have lived here for a very long time and deserve to live in peace."

"Oh, goodness gracious me. But what will I tell the insurance man?" Mr. Akran asked.

Archie smiled and nodded. "What if your car was stolen?"

Everyone looked at Archie and back at the car.

"Dur, Archie. It's right here, and that gargoyle has turned to stone on the roof," Imran said pointing with both hands.

"Well, suppose in the morning, when you get up, it was at the bottom of the loch, never to be seen again. What then?"

Mr. Akran nodded. "But who will be putting the car in loch?"

"Not who. What. I know something that will pick it up drop it in tonight. Anyway, why are you all here?" Archie asked, finally giving Mrs. Akran a welcome hug.

"Happy Christmas, Archie!" Imran smiled and gave Archie a hug.

"Oi! Watch it!" Jock was squashed between the two boys.

"Good point, furry thing. I feel a bit strange hugging Archie while he's dressed in a skirt."

"I'm a sporran not a furry *thing*. And Archie is wearing a Scottish kilt not a skirt," Jock snapped at Imran.

*

The Akran family stayed for two nights at the White Stag Inn. Later that night, Archie went back to the underground cavern and returned Jock. Archie was treated like a hero by the sporrans. Gordon agreed to help and picked up the Akran's family car. Today, if you ever go scuba diving at Loch Ness you may find a crushed and beaten car at the bottom, along with hundreds of concrete gargoyles. It would be a great wonder to onlookers how exactly the objects made its way to the center of the loch before they were dropped.

Of course, Mr. MacGregor tried to keep the secret, until he got drunk and tried to convince local people he had seen the Loch Ness Monster again—along with hundreds of gargoyles and a live sporran. Many told him he was drunk and should go home.

When he was sober, he stopped Archie as he walked past his home. "So, Archie, you convinced your friends to keep the secret of the loch?" Mr. MacGregor said.

Archie gave a tight-lipped smile and nodded.

"Everyone thinks I'm a crazy drunk now, after all I did for you and your sporran."

Archie sighed and walked towards him. "What do you mean *now*? I'm sorry, but most thought that before, and we have to keep it secret else we will have thousands of tourists and scientists here."

Mr. MacGregor sat on a rock and combed his long sideburns with his fingers. Archie sat next to him.

"You know, laddie, in my lifetime I have seen great things get invented. Steam trains, electric trains, cars, the telephone, photographs, phonographs, television, movies, steel ships, the electric light, and the aircraft that fly so effortlessly above our heads.

"I have seen many men come and go. Winston Churchill, Martin Luther King, Elvis Presley, Adolf Hitler, Albert Einstein, The Beatles, and various kings and queens. They all, like me, sweated under the same sun and looked up at the moon with someone we love. I have seen many wars. I have seen plagues and death on a scale that would haunt most. But nothing—nothing—will ever be so formidable as the beast of the loch," Mr. MacGregor croaked.

"You have lived to see all that because of him, because of his bite," Archie said. He felt a strange closeness to Mr. MacGregor. Maybe it was that he too had been scratched by Gordon or maybe because they had shared a great battle on the loch's edge against the gargoyles and the nuckelavee.

*

Christmas Eve arrived. Archie was in a good mood. He sat and watched *The Polar Express* followed by *Elf* on TV. His father was working at the White Stag tonight, so he dressed in a clean shirt and came downstairs. "Come on, Archie. We'd better get going. I have to get to work. You can sleep at the White Stag tonight."

"But it's Christmas tomorrow. Won't we both want to be here in the morning? It's our first Christmas together and the first one without . . ."

"Oh, Christmas. And there I was thinking you didn't care about Christmas." Alec gave Archie a glare.

Archie looked puzzled and tilted his head to one side. "Why did you think that?"

"*Why?* Well, maybe it was something to do with how you left out the back door and missed the Christmas church service. Or maybe how you opened your Christmas present early, leaving the paper and instructions all over the floor and then hid the kite."

Archie's eyes widened. "I—um—oh . . ." The words were forcing themselves from his lips.

"'Um' and 'oh' won't cut it, Archie. I was looking forward to seeing you open your present, and you took that away from me. The whole village goes to church for the Christmas service. Everyone, every faith or no faith. We all go, except *Archie Wilson*, of course. He has better things to do. So I don't see any point in doing anything special for tomorrow, do you?"

Archie was stunned. He had completely forgotten about the kite. He was unsure what to say because he knew his father would not believe the truth. He was stuck. Should he make up a story and lie? No, he had done enough of that. In the end, he did the only thing he felt that was appropriate.

Archie walked up to his father and looked him in the eye. "I'm sorry, Dad." He gave his father a hug for the very first time. Feeling the closeness of his father did something Archie never expected. The thought of hurting his father upset him, but having a hug from someone he now loved moved Archie to tears. He cried his heart out.

Alec was taken back by his son's emotional outburst. He had to fight his own tears. He picked Archie up and kissed him. Archie threw his arms around his father's neck. Finally they became a family unit, a normal family. That's if such a thing exists. A family that gets annoyed at each other, gets on each other's nerves at times, sometimes argues and fights. But deep down, they love each other more than life itself.

Alec never knew what happened to the kite or why Archie often had wet swim shorts hanging in the bathroom. One thing Alec knew for sure was that he was happier now than he had ever been in his life. Having Archie made his life complete.

Archie Wilson's adventures had just begun. When drunk Mr. MacGregor told new stories such as how the nuckelavee had surfaced and how his once biggest enemy, the Loch Ness Monster, had killed it with the help of a ten-year-old boy, of course no one believed him. But, then again, no one really knew what type of boy Archie Wilson was.

Loch Ness and its mysterious secrets had a new protector—someone who would protect the surrounding land and waters at all costs. A mere boy, who despite all the odds had killed the nuckelavee, had become friends of Gordon, the Loch Ness Monster, and the last remaining sporrans. And, of course, the bravest sporran of them all, Jock, who in the face of danger had the nerve to call the nuckelavee a "spawny-eyed pig-faced wazzock." The creatures that lived in the underwater cavern knew that when things went really bad, there was only one person in the world he could really rely on: Archie Wilson.

# Epilogue

The following morning Archie had been awake for at least an hour before the alarm clock beeped. Still, he paused before reaching over to turn it off. With a sigh, he rolled onto his back and yawned. Something was bothering him and he couldn't quite put his finger on it. He pulled himself out of bed and plodded into the bathroom to pee. He looked at his reflection in the mirror. His brown hair stuck up in all directions, just like his father's. Archie wondered if he would end up looking more like his mom or his dad.

Then suddenly a fear shot through his body, a fear that shook him so much he almost wet down his leg. It was a fear far worse than seeing the nuckelavee or being attacked by gargoyles or losing his mom. He leaned forward and gazed deep into the mirror, looking at his round face.

The thought of it was terrifying. *The scratch from Gordon, it gives me powers to be strong and live a long time like Mr. MacGregor. But what if—*

He could barely bring himself to think of it.

*What if I stay a boy age ten-and-a-half forever?*

*More books by* **Mark A. Cooper**

## The Jason Steed Series

'Fledgling' Jason Steed. Book 1

'Revenge' Jason Steed. Book 2

Jason Steed 'Absolutely Nothing'. Book 3

'Royal Decree', Jason Steed. Book 4

'Face-Off'. Jason Steed 5

## The Edelweiss Pirates Series.

Operation Einstein '**Edelweiss Pirates**'. 1

**Edelweiss Pirates'** The Edelweiss Express. 2

## www.markacooper.com

Twitter @AuthorMACooper

Made in the USA
Middletown, DE
17 July 2020